Beneath
Quentaris

THE QUENTARIS CHRONICLES

Beneath Quentaris

Michael Pryor

Lothian
BOOKS

To Sam and Leo Pryor

Thomas C. Lothian Pty Ltd
132 Albert Road, South Melbourne, Victoria 3205
www.lothian.com.au

Visit the Quentaris and Michael Pryor websites!
www.quentaris.com
www.michaelpryor.com.au

First published 2003
Reprinted 2005

National Library of Australia
Cataloguing-in-Publication data:

Pryor, Michael.
Beneath Quentaris

ISBN 0 7344 0556 1 (pbk)

1. Life on other planets — Juvenile fiction.
2. Quests (Expeditions) — Juvenile fiction.
3. Magic — Juvenile fiction.
I. Title. (Series: Quentaris Chronicles).

A823.3

Cover artwork by Marc McBride
Cover and text design by John van Loon
Printed in Australia by Griffin Press

Contents

Nisha Fairsight passed a fireball from hand to hand while she watched children playing in the fountain. The fireball barely felt warm to her and she could only see its pale flame because she had found some shade under an awning. She sat cross-legged, her back to the brick wall, frowning with concentration.

Nisha sighed when the fireball wavered, popped and disappeared. She leaned back, basking in the heat that had baked Quentaris for weeks. The voices of the children came to her from amid the laughter and splashing.

'One and two and three and four,
Queenie went off to the war.
Five and six and seven, eight,
Queenie came back through the gate.'

Nisha smiled at the old rhyme. It took her back to when she was young and her parents were still alive. The few memories she had of this time were precious and she cherished them.

Nisha tried to summon another fireball, but nothing appeared.

During a Zolka invasion barely two months ago, she had learned that her parents hadn't abandoned her in the rift caves. Searching for adventure, they had found danger — and had sacrificed themselves to save their daughter. Understanding this helped Nisha accept her fire-magician heritage and enabled her to help save Quentaris from the Zolka.

But without the guidance of her parents, Nisha's fire-magic power was wayward and difficult to manage. She had practised, but she had trouble keeping even a small fireball burning. She hadn't been able to reproduce the all-consuming flames which had blunted the Zolka invasion.

Nisha rubbed her hands together, feeling a ghostly tingle of heat there. She put her elbows on her knees, her chin in her hands and looked at the children.

The fountain on Tarquin's Hill had recently been rebuilt. The new masonry was clean and grey. A dozen children frolicked in the knee-deep water, letting the water tumble down on them from the spouts above. Wet and giggling, they had joined hands and continued the old rhyme:

'North and south and east and west,
Queenie laid them all to rest.
Round about and up and down,
Queenie bound them to the town.'

Nisha smiled as the rest of the rhyme was lost in shrieking and splashing. She wanted to join them, but she felt that fourteen was simply too old for such play. Instead, she leaned back against the wall and watched the fountain and the ripples of heat which rose from the pavement all around.

Suddenly, the ground beneath her began to shake like a gently tapped gong. The children in the fountain broke off from their playing, but the trembling stopped quickly. Soon, they were back to their singing and water games.

Nisha admired the way the children had grown so accustomed to the tremors from under the city. There had been so many in recent months that people simply waited for each to settle. Some broken mugs, some frightened animals, a few cracks in walls, was all the damage the tremors had caused. She smiled when she remembered that just this morning, the warning bells on the town walls had rung all over the west side of town. It had taken some time before people realised that it was another tremor shaking the bells, not those on watch duty.

Nisha stretched out, hands behind her head. She enjoyed the heat.

Chapter Two

Tal & the Stranger

T AL tapped his drum with a dreary beat as the sun glared down from a cloudless sky. Then he wiped the sweat from his brow. Even though he was crouched in a patch of shade thrown by one of the pillars, the Square of Dreams was like a griddle. Tal grinned. He was sure he could fry an egg out there. And he was certain he wouldn't have any trouble from anyone stepping on such an egg. The Square of

Dreams was as empty as a miser's heart. Tal was resigned to earning no coins from his music today.

Tal had never known Quentaris to have been so hot for so long. It had been months since rain had visited the city and days since a cloud had marred the sky. The heat had sunk into the stones of the city, into laneways, walls and buildings. Few people could walk the streets barefooted.

It was no use, Tal decided. He stowed his drumsticks in his pouch and strapped the drum to his back. A patter of dust stirred at the base of the pillar as the hot air roused itself a little. Tal thought of going to the Old Tree Guesthouse and seeing if Nisha was there. They could go down into the cellar, where it was a little cooler, and rest among the kegs and barrels.

'You've given up, boy?'

Tal looked up. 'You wish a tune, sir?' he said, shading his eyes.

'I think I can live without a tune from a drum,' the stranger said dryly. He was wearing rich clothes of an old-fashioned cut. He was thin, with a forked beard stretching to his chest. Even through his heat weariness, Tal was impressed by the stranger's beard. It was a striking colour. At first, Tal thought it was golden, then he thought it was silver. Then he realised it rippled with both gold and silver, like a river reflecting sunlight. 'I'm merely after directions.'

'Ask away. I know Quentaris better than most.'

'The Old Tree Guesthouse. Do you know it?'

'Of course! I was about to go there myself, to see my friend.'

'Ah. This would be Nisha, would it?'

'You know Nisha?'

The stranger nodded slightly. 'I've been looking for her for some time. She's an untrained fire magician, isn't she?'

Tal chewed his lip. 'She might be,' he said slowly. 'But with no family, it's hard for her to realise her heritage.'

'So she would appreciate any help she could find.'

'Well, I suppose that's true.'

'I know of something that may help her in this time of trial.'

'Nisha would be grateful, sir, if you could help her.'

The stranger smiled briefly. 'It is not me who can

help her, lad. It is you.' He gestured in the direction of the rift caves. 'I have knowledge of a certain arte-fact that can help young Nisha in her passage towards true magicianhood. In one of the rift caves, it is, but not for long.'

'Not for long?'

'If this artefact is not found within half an hour, the minor rift that has exposed it will disappear and it will be lost forever. I would get it myself, but I have other business to attend to.'

Tal got to his feet. The stranger's story wasn't wholly convincing, but Tal badly wanted to help Nisha. After the cheers had died down following the defeat of the Zolka, Nisha had grown morose and melancholy. Even with old Stanas' advice, she found it hard to control her power. In a trial, she had attempted to shape a cooking fire, but it went sadly awry, scorching the fireplace and the wall around it. Brooding over this, Nisha had confided in Tal that she desperately wanted to master her fire magic, to honour the memory of her parents, but feared she would never reach her goal. She looked so dejected that it had plucked at Tal's heart.

Tal shrugged. The stranger may have subtle plans — but if that were true, he would simply be like most people in Quentaris.

'Tell me where it is,' Tal said, making a silent vow to make 'careful' his watchword, and 'cunning' his middle name.

Chapter Three

Arna blew a wisp of hair from her mouth as she juggled a tray full of mugs and tankards. 'Nisha! Can you find Stanas, please? We need some more help here in the taproom.' With that, the proprietor of the Old Tree Guesthouse turned back to the patrons who had come looking for cool beer.

The Old Tree had always been a popular destination for both locals and travellers. Its lodgings were renowned for comfort and reasonable prices, and many adventurers chose to stay there before daring the perils of the rift caves. Merchants, too, attracted to Quentaris by the trade and exotic goods that resulted from the presence of the rift caves, enjoyed the Old Tree.

The locals, however, simply enjoyed the food and drink. Arna was a talented chef, and even though she spent less time in the kitchen these days, due to her duties as manager, she always employed skilful under-chefs. The beer, too, was famous, and this was the work of old Stanas.

Stanas was a water magician, but one who had renounced his powers. Many years ago, he had accidentally caused a huge wave to roll down the Quentaris River, and it had drowned his wife and children. Broken by this, he was a shattered man until Arna took him in as stable manager. Her kindness was rewarded when Stanas gradually began to assemble the basic necessities for a brewery. He set up in the disused cellar, and somehow was able to find a spring of pure water in a corner of that gloomy space. This water became the source of the best beer in Quentaris and slowly Stanas began to trust his powers again. And so he was able to use them to help Nisha repel the Zolka invaders.

Nisha wiped her hands on her apron and hurried towards the cellar. 'Stanas! Are you down there?'

Nisha scowled when she received no answer. She was sure Stanas was growing harder of hearing. It left her no choice but to go down into the cellar. She stood at the top of the stairs, rubbing her hands together and chewing her lip.

It wasn't the blackness that made Nisha nervous. The cellar wasn't all that dark, to tell the truth. Small windows high in the walls actually looked out onto the street. Even though the glass was the cheapest, enough light filtered into the cellar to make it dim rather than dark.

No, it was the fact that the cellar reminded Nisha of her encounter with the earth elemental, just before the Zolka invasion. The stairs, the enclosed space, all took her back to the narrow escape from the rampaging monster. She found it hard to breathe, as if all the air had vanished.

Nisha took one step, then she paused. Her heart was beating rapidly. The gloom below seemed deeper, more threatening. She wanted to go and find a lantern, but knew that once she turned back up the stairs, it would be even harder to go down again.

Suddenly, she had an idea. She closed her eyes and concentrated. Holding out her hand, she called a small fireball into being. When it appeared, her fire-magician heritage meant it barely felt warm.

Nisha opened her eyes, grinned, and held the fireball up high. All the shadows fled and she marched down the stairs. The little fireball burned with a clear yellow light, and it made Nisha's heart easy. Her breathing was freer now, and the warm, yeasty smell of the cellar was cheering. 'Stanas! Where are you? Arna needs help in the taproom.'

Near the bottom of the stairs was the first vat. It was bubbling gently as the wort began to ferment. Curious, Nisha leaned over the stair rail to peer into the malty liquid, knowing this was the beginning of beer.

At that moment, the little fireball flickered. Nisha turned in time to see the fireball bounce up and down on her hand. 'No,' she said, as if to a naughty child. 'Stop that.'

The fireball continued to bounce. Then it shimmered and started to lose its rich yellow colour.

Pulses of brown and red blinked across its surface.

Then it began to feel hot.

Nisha was surprised. In all her efforts with fire-balls since her power had awoken, they had never felt hot before. They were always cool, like a soft breeze. She started to close her hand, and the fireball squirted out between her fingers like a cake of wet soap.

Nisha watched, open-mouthed, as the flickering fireball fell gently towards the vat. When it touched the surface, it vanished with a flare of light and a sour hiss. A burnt smell filled the cellar, and Nisha coughed.

Old Stanas appeared from the shadows. He looked up at Nisha and he shook his head. His face was sad as he patted the side of the vat. 'We'll have to dump this batch, we will. And give it a good clean out. It's spoiled, now.'

'I'm sorry, Stanas, truly I am. It was the fireball.'

Stanas sighed and looked at Nisha. 'I thought as much, Nisha. It's a rough magic you have.'

Nisha's face crumpled. She wanted to cry. 'I know, Stanas. I know.'

Chapter Four

The Cliff & the Caves

TAL stood and watched the workers mending the great gates in the wall by the Last and First Station. Woodworkers and masons laboured in teams, endeavouring to repair the damage done in the last Zolka invasion. Metalworkers strapped great bands of yanlen onto the gates to strengthen them, confident that the mysterious material from the rift caves would resist any attack. The Archon of

Quentaris had complained loudly about the cost, then he simply imposed an extra tax on the merchants. They in turn wailed and whined, and — with sad faces and much wringing of hands — raised their prices. The citizens of Quentaris saw the higher prices, shrugged, and suffered. In the end, the gates were rebuilt.

The soldiers on duty at the Last and First Station all knew Tal and nodded or waved to him. He was one of the many who enjoyed watching the adventurers, caravans and wagon trains that entered or came from the rift caves. Most of the traffic was humdrum and ordinary, the guides brisk and business-like, but there was always a chance that something exotic would pass by.

Tal had often lounged in the shade of the walls. He'd seen heroes and merchants pass by. He'd seen wagons, horses, camels and donkeys, all laden with goods, treasure and high hopes. He'd seen sad-eyed strangers, whole families of them, trudge from the caves, the dispossessed.

But he'd never been into the rift caves himself. Tal always had a healthy respect for them. He'd seen adventurers boldly march into caves and never return. He'd seen others stagger back to the city, wounded and crushed in spirit, whispering of strange worlds and stranger creatures. His minstrel friends gossiped of whole companies vanishing and stories of parties lost in rifts were the subject of many a late-night discussion.

Over the years, Tal had told himself that staying away from the caves was wise. Now, as he stood inside the gate and studied the vast cliff, Tal realised his heart was beating a rapid rhythm. Heat rose from the cobblestones around him and he wiped sweat from his forehead.

Tier on tier of oft-trodden paths led into openings in the rock face. All were well known after generations of exploration. Once inside, other passages and openings led to the rifts themselves. Some swore that the inner passages and caves shifted and changed. Others felt that new openings and rifts were coming into being all the time. Maps were only useful for a short time, but this didn't prevent silver-tongued hawkers from selling maps to starry-eyed adventurers on their way to the caves.

Tal took a deep breath and felt the hot air harsh in his nose and throat. He sought out the small cave entrance on the third level, next to a large opening that had half-collapsed. The stranger had been firm that this was the way for Tal to follow.

Tal didn't give himself time for his nervousness to grow into fear. A merchant astride a white horse, with two well-armed professionals from the Bodyguards' Guild, was heading through the gate and towards the caves. A bored-looking guide led the way. Tal waited for them to pay their toll, then tossed the guard a silver moon. In return, he got a grin and a wave, and then he, too, was on his way.

Tal paused for a moment, letting his eyes become used to the dim light in the cave. He tried to listen hard, ready for any menace that might be lurking. He knew that the caves were usually safe this close to the outside world, but creatures had been known to blunder from rifts and waylay the unwary. Of course, there were other dangers too — sly humans, elves or other races. Anyone in the rift caves was advised to be suspicious, alert and well-armed.

Tal touched the knife at his belt. It was the only weapon he had. He knew he wasn't skillful enough with anything else to make a difference. Besides, a razor-sharp broadsword might make him walk a little taller, but with only a knife he would be more likely to run than to fight. And, probably, survive.

Fifty good paces inside the cave mouth, the fire magician had said. Then up a rockfall to a rough tunnel. The rift was supposed to be at the end of the tunnel. Tal peered through the gloom. He could see the ledge formed by the rockfall and he thought he could make out the tunnel. He took a deep breath and slipped into the cave, keeping close to the rock wall.

Tal moved carefully, not hurrying, not dawdling. There was no sign of foot traffic or wheels on the floor of the cave. Tal guessed it didn't lead to a rich world, at least, not at the moment. Tal knew some rifts shifted and changed, and today's portal to a world full of desirable spices could be tomorrow's portal to a desert world full of aggressive monsters.

The sounds of the city died as Tal moved further into the cave. The shouts and cries of street sellers, the ringing of hammers on anvils, the rumble of carts on cobblestoned roads, all faded away. Instead, the silence of the cave wrapped itself around Tal. Even though the air was cool on his skin after the heat outside, Tal didn't want to linger. He moved more quickly and mounted the rockfall in a few strides.

Halfway up the slope, the earth shuddered underfoot. Tal spread his arms, seeking balance, but the tremor soon subsided, grumbling. He listened for falling rock, but heard nothing.

Tal paused at the entrance to the tunnel on hands and knees. A telltale green glow hinted at the rift at the other end. Tal slipped his knife from its sheath and held it in one hand. He knew it would make crawling awkward, but if anything attacked him in the tunnel, a sheathed knife would be useless.

The tunnel was a tight squeeze, even for someone of Tal's compact size. He grimaced as he lost some skin from his shoulders squirming through the rough entrance, but he crawled on.

The green glow was closer than he expected. Tal sheathed his knife and studied the rift for a moment, the first he had ever actually seen.

Judging by the tales of returning travellers, this was a small rift. Many were large enough for a wagon and its harness beasts. Others were large enough for a human to walk through. Some — like this one — were tiny.

It was a wavy line of light, hanging like a split in air. Tal could clearly see the tunnel continuing behind it. A traveller had once told Tal to think of a rift as a seam, a seam between the world of Quentaris and another world. A seam that could be eased apart to allow passage.

This rift was only a few handspans in height. Tal had heard of rift fishers, those who specialised in these tiny rifts. They probed them with long rods, with hooks or sticky mesh on the ends, occasionally retrieving valuable items.

The stranger had been firm that no such equipment was needed for this rift. Tal merely had to reach in and feel around. The world on the other side was hardly a world at all. 'A pocket-sized world,' the stranger had said, 'nothing to fear.'

Tal never believed it when someone told him he had nothing to fear. He knew he had to reach in through the rift and feel around. But if that was all, why were his palms sweating and his hands shaking? His mouth was suddenly dry. What if he were plunging his hand into fire? Or acid? Or worse? Slimy, poisonous creatures were his secret fear and in his mind he could already feel his fingers brushing against something which wrapped tentacles around him and wouldn't let go, before lancing a venomous stinger into his hand.

Tal shook his head. This wouldn't do. At first he considered easing in his hand, hoping to avoid the attention of anything harmful, but then shrugged. Boldness brings rewards, he decided.

Tal reached for the rift, then plunged his hand through.

It was cool on the other side, even cooler than in the rift cave. Tal could feel rock and dust, but nothing else. He ran his fingers over the rocks, which were smooth and the size of hens' eggs. Carefully, he pushed one aside and felt underneath, but only touched more dust.

The dust was fine, almost greasy when he rubbed it between his fingers.

Tal leaned forward, frowning with concentration, and his arm passed through to the elbow. A few moments of futile exploration led him to stretch so that his arm disappeared almost entirely into the rift.

At that moment, Tal felt something through the stones in the rift. It was faint at first, but soon began to grow stronger. A vibration, as if something heavy had fallen to the ground. Then it was repeated, then again, growing stronger. Soon, the stones were jumping, and he could feel the dust rising and falling as well. *Thump, thump, thump, thump*.

Footsteps. Tal was sure of it.

The stones began to jostle against each other as the footsteps came faster and heavier. He gritted his teeth as the stones clashed and pinched his fingers. The footsteps felt nearer and he could clearly hear the sound leaking through the rift. It was the sound of something massive and it was rapidly coming closer.

Suddenly, he felt something — something that wasn't rock or dust. It was metal.

Tal quickly seized the metal object. He whipped back his hand, but as he did he felt a feather-light touch, something hard and sharp, then his arm was back through the rift and it closed behind him.

When Tal looked at the object in his hand, he realised he held a large silver spoon. Then, numbly, he realised that a trickle of blood was dripping from a long, thin scratch on the back of his hand.

Tal shuddered at his narrow escape.

Chapter Five

'Tell me again, Tal, why would I want a spoon?'

'Nisha, there must be something about this spoon. The stranger told me exactly where to find it.'

'But a spoon?'

Nisha turned back to her job. She took her pole and used it to stir and pound the tablecloths in the copper boiler. Steam billowed around her and she waved it away.

Nisha saw how Tal stood in the doorway of the

wash-house, unwilling to brave the heat from the row of washing boilers. She didn't blame him. She seemed to be the only one who could manage to work in the wash-house for any length of time. But the Old Tree Guesthouse needed tablecloths, so the laundry had to be done — despite the hot weather.

Tal wiped his sweaty brow. 'Maybe it's a magic spoon,' he finally ventured.

Nisha sighed. The scarf binding her hair had slipped and she leaned the laundry pole against the wall before retying it. She knew Tal was trying to help. 'A magic spoon,' she repeated. 'I'm sorry, Tal. It doesn't sound right to me.'

'What do you mean?'

'Magic should be grand and mysterious. A spoon is too ordinary to be magical.'

'There's magic in ordinary things, too,' Tal said firmly. 'If you know where to look.'

'Here, give me the spoon. Let me see it.'

Nisha studied the spoon. Made of a light, silvery metal, it was larger than a teaspoon, but smaller than a tablespoon. The bowl was round and the handle looked as if it was made of three strands of metal woven together in a braid.

'It's a pretty thing,' Nisha said. 'But I can't see anything magical about it.'

'It doesn't *feel* magical to you?' Tal's face was disappointed.

Nisha held the handle tightly, then she stroked the metal with her fingertips. 'I can't feel anything. Of course, perhaps a *real* magician would,' she added bitterly.

'Don't say things like that. Have you forgotten who saved Quentaris with her magic?'

Nisha smiled a little. 'Thank you, Tal. But your mysterious stranger seems to have been playing a joke on you.' She held out the spoon.

'A strange sort of joke.' Tal reached for the spoon. As he went to grasp it, he fumbled. When he tried to catch it, the spoon fell to the stone floor of the washhouse.

It struck the flagstones. Both Tal and Nisha were amazed when a voice like moonlight on silver filled the air. 'I belong to Alberic Mallison,' the spoon sang. 'Please return me.'

Nisha stared at the spoon lying on the floor. 'What was that?'

'Magic. It must be magic.' Tal squatted and

studied the spoon. Carefully, he picked it up. 'It doesn't look damaged.'

'Will it do it again?'

Tal shrugged, then dropped the spoon to the flag-stones again. Once more, the shimmering voice rang out: 'I belong to Alberic Mallison. Please return me.'

'Did you notice?' Nisha said. 'The voice wasn't as loud that time.'

Tal nodded. 'The spoon didn't fall as far.' He picked it up. 'I have an idea.'

Tal held the end of the handle and struck the stone floor. Immediately, the spoon again informed them that it belonged to Alberic Mallison and wished to be returned.

Tal looked up at Nisha and grinned. 'It's like a tuning fork, but it's a spoon. Watch.'

Tal tapped the spoon on the floor again: 'I belong to Alberic Mallison. Please return me.'

'I can feel it vibrate,' Tal said.

'How clever! But who is Alberic Mallison?'

Tal stood. 'I've never heard of him. Perhaps old Stanas knows.'

They found Stanas wiping down the long bar in the main taproom. 'I've heard of Alberic Mallison,' he said. 'But it was a long time ago.'

'Tell us about him,' Nisha said.

Stanas wiped his hands on his apron. 'I should be tending the bar. Arna won't be happy.'

'You can do that and still talk to us. We won't scare off the customers.'

'No, you won't do that. They're not going to leave here and brave the heat outside.'

Nisha knew that the taproom was hot as an oven, but with shutters over the windows, the darkness gave the illusion of coolness. Four or five leather-workers were seated at a bench near the wall and three bodyguards were near the unused fireplace, speaking in low voices and nursing drinks.

'Here, you may as well drink while you listen.' Stanas poured two mugs of lemon cordial from an earthenware jug. It was cold, the water having just been brought up from the spring in the cellar.

'Thank you, Stanas,' Tal said. 'Now, who is Alberic Mallison?'

'If I remember correctly, he made the best cutlery anyone had ever seen.'

'Knives, forks and spoons?' Nisha ventured.

'And ladles, servers and slicers. He was the master.'

'Could he have made this?' Tal held out the magical spoon.

Stanas smiled, his eyes bright and interested. 'It looks like a Mallison. But there's only one way of knowing.'

Stanas took the spoon and tapped it on the counter. The sweet voice leaped into the air and all of the patrons turned towards it. 'I belong to Alberic Mallison. Please return me.'

Stanas nodded. 'I'd say that's a genuine Mallison. No question about that.'

'It sounds as if he wants his spoon back. Or it wants to go back,' Nisha said.

'Where can we find him?' Tal asked. 'Where does he live? Does he have a workshop, or a shop somewhere?'

Stanas rubbed his chin and gazed up at the ceiling. 'Let me see now. I read about Alberic Mallison. His shop in Graveney Street was famous for his cutlery. But that was five hundred years ago.'

'Five hundred years ago?' Nisha burst out. 'What good is that?'

'Well,' Stanas said. 'You know how these things are. In Quentaris, five hundred years is nothing. This guesthouse has been here for twice that. Parts of it, at least. Why don't you go to Graveney Street and see if his family still runs a cutlery business?'

Tal looked puzzled. 'I thought I knew every street in the city, but I've never heard of Graveney Street.'

'Nor have I,' Nisha added.

'Hmm? Well, some streets in Quentaris have a habit of wandering around, but I expect you know that.' He scratched his head. 'Graveney Street, Graveney Street. I think it was in Lower Quentaris. Yes, I'm sure of it. Lower Quentaris.'

'By the river?' Nisha asked.

'No, not by the river. Lower Quentaris. The undertown.'

'Sorry, Stanas,' Nisha said. 'But I've never heard of it.'

Stanas blinked. 'Not heard of Lower Quentaris?' Then he stopped and looked thoughtful. 'Tal?'

Tal looked uncomfortable. 'I've been there.'

'See? Tal knows of it.' Stanas picked up his cloth and began mopping the counter.

Nisha crossed her arms impatiently. 'Well, what is

this place? Stop being so mysterious.'

'I've only been there once.' Tal paused. 'Do you remember me telling you of Esbandalon, one of the oldest musicians? He taught me much about Quentaris, and musicianship, and fellowship.'

Nisha had heard this wistfulness in Tal's voice before, especially when talking of Esbandalon and the rough-and-ready crew that was Quentaris minstrelsy. An orphan, Tal had been raised by the troubadours, musicians and entertainers from an early age. Esbandalon the harpist was the closest to a father that Tal had ever known.

'Esbandalon told you of Lower Quentaris?' Nisha asked.

'He *showed* me Lower Quentaris. It was part of my education, he said.'

'Wise man, Esbandalon,' Stanas muttered, without looking up from his work of mopping the counter.

'But what *is* it?' Nisha asked.

'It's a city under the city,' Tal said. 'There are streets, shops, houses, all under what we know as Quentaris. It's been there for a long time. Some say the oldest parts of Quentaris are down there.'

'How did it get there?'

'Esbandalon didn't know. He said that some tell of a flood, where parts of the city sank and were over-built later. Others say that people simply put up buildings on top of buildings, and then cunning sorts tunnelled from forgotten basement to forgotten basement, eventually creating a town under the ground. Some parts of the undertown are quite grand, with proper streets and buildings, just like above ground. But further away from the centre of Lower Quentaris the undertown is more like a series of tunnels and caves.' He sighed. 'We didn't stay long. Esbandalon didn't think it was safe.'

'Well, that's true,' Stanas agreed as he wrung his cloth into a bucket. 'Normal rules often don't apply in the undertown. I think you should stay away from it.'

'But we have to take the spoon back to its owner,' Nisha protested. 'Tal?'

Tal frowned. 'Stanas is probably right,' he said slowly. 'It's a strange place.'

Nisha picked up the spoon and weighed it in her hand.

'Treat it as a curiosity, a keepsake,' Stanas suggested. 'It's a lovely piece.'

'A curiosity. That it is,' said Nisha softly.

Chapter Six

Below & Beneath

T HE next day, when the sun was barely above the horizon, Nisha went walking, alone. She often did this, when the city was waking up. It gave her a chance to think as her feet took her through the lanes, the alleys and the streets. As she pondered and mused, she could walk for miles and miles before breakfast.

This particular morning, Quentaris was just starting to bustle, with workers making their way to tanneries, forges and mills. The Dung Brigade was doing its best to clear the streets before they became full of citizens. The weary members of the Watch nightshift stood on street corners, propping themselves up against walls and in doorways.

Nisha had the magical spoon in her pocket, and she held it as she strode along, wondering what she was going to do. The more she thought about the undertown, the more she wanted to see it. A whole city under the one she knew? Her curiosity wouldn't allow her to ignore the chance to explore it! Nisha smiled. Lower Quentaris would be a fine refuge from the heat. It had to be cool and shady, she was sure of it!

Nisha stopped and looked around at where she found herself. She vaguely remembered crossing High Street, somewhere near the Square of Dreams. All she could see were the backs of shops. The buildings looming over the lane made her feel as if she were at the bottom of a deep chasm.

Suddenly, Nisha felt a tap on her shoulder. 'You look lost. Can I help?'

She turned to find a small lad. He was young, perhaps seven or eight years old, and he was studying her with a half smile on his face. His eyes were clear and bright blue, and his hair was a startling golden mop, covering his ears and reaching to the base of his neck. As he cocked his head, his hair jigged, and Nisha saw it was full of silver streaks.

'Thank you,' Nisha said, 'but I'm on my way home.'

She started to leave, but the boy took her arm. 'Home? Wouldn't you rather see Lower Quentaris?'

Nisha stared at him. 'What did you say?'

'Lower Quentaris, the undertown, I can show it all to you! I can guide you and keep you safe, or my name isn't Damino!'

Nisha removed Damino's hand from her arm and looked carefully at the boy. There were many children who seemed to make the streets their home, begging or running errands for copper coins. Damino could be one of them.

But his appearing here so neatly, just when she had made up her mind to seek Lower Quentaris, made her uneasy. His appearance, too, gave her pause. It was as if there was something not quite right about the boy. She sensed that there was a touch of magic about him. Treading quietly was the best plan here, she decided.

'If it's money that's concerning you,' Damino hurried on, 'I can wait for my payment! You can pay me what you think I'm worth once we're done. What can be fairer than that?'

Damino's simple greed reassured Nisha. 'Done. Lead on, Damino!'

'This way!' He bounded past Nisha and ran to the end of the laneway. There, deep in the shadows thrown by the overhanging buildings, was a heap of bricks and stone.

'Our way to Lower Quentaris,' Damino announced, and he pointed at a large hole. He didn't wait for Nisha. He leapt down the hole like a grasshopper.

Nisha went more slowly. After easing herself through the hole and scrambling over a few yards of fallen stone, she was surprised to see stairs leading downwards. Damino stood there, beckoning. 'This way! This way!' Lanterns glowed some distance below and Damino bobbed down the stairs.

The stairway opened onto a narrow street. Nisha stopped, her mouth open. Crooked buildings crowded together on either side of the cobblestoned street. Some were two and even three low storeys, disappearing into stone above. Wooden beams and stone columns were spaced irregularly, a forest holding up the rock and earth above. On almost all the columns, brackets held lamps and lanterns. The result was soft, uneven, guttering light, with many shadows lingering in corners. To Nisha's eyes, the scene was like late evening, just before true night has fallen. She could make out the figures of a few people, flitting among the shadows, but otherwise the street was deserted.

As she stood, taking in the underground scene, something niggled at her, something that made Lower Quentaris quite unlike its above-ground counterpart.

Then she had it. 'It's quiet,' she said to herself. Quentaris itself was a constant hubbub of noise. The undertown was hushed, muffled, waiting.

Nisha looked around but couldn't see Damino anywhere. 'Damino,' she called, but she was afraid to raise her voice in this place. The warnings of Stanas and Tal echoed in her mind as she stood uncertainly. She looked over her shoulder at the stairway leading back to the street above. Then she shook her head. 'No,' she said aloud, and she found the spoon and drew it from her pocket. 'I'm taking you home. Now, which way is Graveney Street?'

It took some time to find her way. The first passer-by that Nisha approached hurried off, crossing the street as she drew nearer. The next was walking along, brandishing a long rapier and talking to himself. Nisha crossed the street this time, to avoid him. After that, the only pedestrians she saw vanished into buildings before she could hail them.

Nisha stopped under a tall iron lamp-post. Three lanterns hung from it like softly glowing fruit. Well, what now? she wondered.

Suddenly, Damino came around the corner of a low building on the other side of the street. 'Ah, there you are! Where have you been?'

Nisha blinked. 'I haven't been anywhere. It was you who left.'

Damino shrugged. 'I was only gone a moment. I had people to see.'

'Ah.' Nisha put a finger to her lips. She wanted to ask who Damino was seeing in the undertown, but she quelled her curiosity. 'Can you take me to Graveney Street?'

'Graveney Street? It's north of here! Follow me!'

Chapter Seven

Cutlery & its Maker

GRAVENEY Street was short and narrow. Two massive wooden columns stood in the middle of it, both with ornate metalwork lanterns. Half a dozen shabby buildings lined the street and it didn't take long before Nisha found one with a small sign on the door — 'Mallison'.

Nisha put her face to the window. A curtain of cobwebs hung on the inside of the window, and all she could see were dark, unmoving shapes. She straightened and wiped dust from her hands.

After weighing up her options, Nisha rapped sharply at the door. No-one answered. She tried again, but the knocking sounded as if it died as soon as it entered the room beyond.

She tried the latch and found the door wasn't locked.

Nisha chewed her lip a little. If she simply walked in, she could be mistaken for a thief. And who knew what they did to thieves in the undertown?

But she couldn't simply turn around and go home. How would she sleep at night, knowing she'd run away with the mystery of the magical spoon unsolved?

'Damino,' she said, over her shoulder, 'do you know this shop well?'

When there was no answer, Nisha looked around to find that Damino had vanished. 'A strange sort of guide,' she whispered to herself.

Nisha took a deep breath, pushed the door open and took a step inside. 'Hello? Is this the cutler's?'

The air inside the shop was still and dry, and it felt heavy, as if it had been undisturbed for a long time. Nisha stopped a few paces into the darkened room.

'Hello?' she called. 'Is anyone there?'

At that moment, light flared in the darkness.

'Ah, welcome,' said a voice. As the light grew, Nisha could make out a tall, frail-looking man adjusting a lantern. His elbows and knees stood out knobbily, and a great plume of white hair swept back from his head. He rubbed his eyes sleepily and stared at her. 'What can I do for you?'

Nisha's palms felt clammy and she rubbed them together. 'I'm looking for Alberic Mallison, the cutler. Am I in the right place?'

The old man spread his hands. 'Look around, young lady. Does it seem like you are in the right place?'

Behind wooden-topped counters, the walls were lined with shelves and they displayed enough glittering cutlery for an army.

Nisha saw knives, forks and spoons in a hundred different styles and finishes. Some had handles of bone, others of metal or glass. A few had handles that looked as if they had been carved from coloured gemstones. She recognised silver, brass and steel, but also saw knives with pearly blades like hammered moonlight, spoons with dancing rainbow sheens and forks that were midnight black. Intricate patterns, smooth contours and hard, geometric shapes could all be found on the shelves. And not just knives, forks and spoons. Proudly displayed were tongs, eating sticks, ladles, servers and dozens of other items that Nisha couldn't put a name to. What was the thing that looked like three squat spirals set in a handle, for instance?

Nisha wanted to spend hours, days, even months gazing at the array of beautifully crafted items, but she turned back to the old man behind the counter. He was watching her closely.

Nisha gathered herself. 'This is the shop that once belonged to Alberic Mallison?'

'Indeed. And it still does.'

'It does?'

'Of course. I am known as Alberic Mallison.'

Nisha stared, but then realised that this wasn't unlikely. Many families passed names down through the generations. This Alberic Mallison must be the great-great-great grandson of the original Alberic Mallison.

'Oh. I'm Nisha Fairsight. I think I have something for you.'

The shopkeeper smiled slightly. 'I see. And what could it be?'

Nisha reached into her pocket and pulled out the magical spoon. 'Here.'

Nisha tapped the spoon on the counter, and the familiar silvery voice rang out: 'I belong to Alberic Mallison. Please return me.'

The shopkeeper went pale. He seemed to have trouble standing and he put both hands on the counter to steady himself. 'Oh my. I had given up hope of ever seeing this again.'

'You know it?'

'I made this spoon,' the shopkeeper said solemnly.

'But you can't have,' Nisha said. 'Stanas told me Alberic Mallison lived five hundred years ago.'

The shopkeeper looked down and sighed. 'Oh yes, it's certainly been five hundred years. Five hundred long years. Now, young lady, may I have my spoon?'

Stunned, Nisha held it out.

'Ah,' Alberic breathed as he cradled his lost spoon in both hands. 'My missing masterpiece!'

'How did you lose it?' Nisha asked.

Alberic rubbed his eyes with the back of his hand. It came away wet. 'So long ago,' he said. He looked up and it was almost as if he had forgotten Nisha was there. 'Come into my workshop.'

The room was neat and tidy, with tools hanging on racks over long wooden benches. Bundles of metal wire were stacked against one wall, next to a large iron chest, and a small hearth was set into another. Alberic pointed to a stool, then busied himself at the hearth before drawing up a chair himself.

'You are the first to come to my premises in years,' the old man said.

'Why?' Nisha asked. 'Your cutlery is wonderful!'

'Once, long ago, it was. I could pick and choose my customers as my skill was in much demand. My cutlery graced the tables of kings and queens and a thousand regal banquets, as well as the homes of the honest and humble.'

Alberic sighed, then stood and went to the hearth. He busied himself with tea-making, then handed a mug to Nisha and pushed a sugar bowl towards her.

'This happened five hundred years ago?' Nisha asked. She saw a small spoon on the workbench, helped herself to sugar and stirred her tea thoughtfully.

'More than that,' Alberic said. He sipped his tea, then stared at the steam rising from the mug. 'And far away from here, in the land of Phrasis. I plied my trade and made wares that fitted the needs of people perfectly, and brought honest joy to them.'

'What happened?'

'I was taken from my home by your Queen Hermia and brought here against my will. And ever since, something has vanished from my craft.'

'What do you mean?' Nisha said. She stopped stirring and tapped the spoon on the rim of the mug. Without warning, the mug cracked, then fell apart. Before Nisha could move, she had a lap full of hot tea.

For an instant, she felt the scalding liquid, but then her heart of fire woke and, immediately, her skin felt cool and untroubled.

'Are you all right?' the old man said, getting to his feet.

'Yes. Just wet.'

'Here,' Alberic said, handing her a cloth. Then he

bent and plucked the spoon from the pool of tea on the wooden floor. 'You used this?' he asked Nisha.

'Oh, I'm sorry. Wasn't I meant to?'

Alberic closed his fist on the spoon. 'It's what I was talking about. Anything I make now is cursed. Try as I might, I cannot make anything that does not cause ill.'

Nisha stared at the spoon. All she had done was tap the mug and yet it had fallen apart in her hands as if the spoon had been a hammer.

'And this curse began when you came to Quentaris?' Nisha wiped her hands on the cloth, then dabbed at her dress.

'When I came to Quentaris, the spoon you found was taken from me. I have been incomplete ever since and my craft has been soured.' Alberic put his mug on the bench and seemed lost in his thoughts for a moment before going on. 'People in Quentaris had heard of my skill, and I made great sets of cutlery for them — proud, glittering sets. But table knives found ways to slip and cut the user. Forks splintered or jabbed cheeks and tongues. Meals were full of discord and argument where once my work had brought contentment. Blood was spilled.'

'One missing spoon did all that?'

'That spoon belonged to the finest set I ever made, the last thing I completed before I was taken from my home. It belonged to the Great Canteen.'

'What's a canteen?' Nisha asked. 'I know of the water-flask called a canteen, but I'm sure that's not what you mean.'

'No, indeed. A cutlery canteen is a case which holds a complete cutlery set — knives, forks, spoons, and the other pieces necessary for a perfectly appointed table. For six people, it may be hundreds of pieces. And in my ambition I wasn't about to limit myself to six people. I aimed to create a complete canteen for two dozen people. It was to have almost a thousand individual items.'

'A thousand,' Nisha echoed. Distantly, she felt the skin beneath her sodden dress glow with warmth. Soon, she was sure, her dress would be dry.

'Each item was to be a work of art, crafted by my own hands with all the care and skill I could give it. Each a small piece of perfection. As such, I knew that I could only use the last of the singing metal.' He looked at Nisha's blank face. 'Singing metal? You've not heard of it? Well, it has been a long time since there has been any in the world. I had some, the last of it there was — and I used it all. Feather-light it was, and with the right art it could be given a voice, as you've heard with the spoon. But singing metal is fiendishly hard to work, and it takes supreme skill to work it well.'

'And what happened?'

'I did it,' Alberic said simply. 'I completed the perfect canteen, the Great Canteen. Each piece was as light as air, but sat solidly in the hand nonetheless. I even made the case myself, something I had never done before. A case of smooth, unmarked metal, unadorned in any way, as I wanted nothing to take away from the glory that was the cutlery itself.'

Nisha watched how Alberic's eyes lit as he described the Great Canteen. His hands moved as he told of each item, as if he were making them all over again. As he did, she could see the younger man he had been, so many years ago. She saw how keenly he felt for something she had always thought of as ordinary. She knew she would never look at knives and forks the same way again.

'But,' Alberic continued, 'I had barely completed it before I was brought here — and the spoon disappeared. Through great magic, I was bound to the undertown of Quentaris, with my Great Canteen ruined. Such a small missing piece, but because of it, my masterwork was as nothing and my skill was tainted.'

Alberic then looked at Nisha and seemed to come to a decision. He stood and went over to the large iron chest. He took a key out of his pocket, opened the chest and beckoned. 'Come, I'll show you the Great Canteen.'

Almost filling the iron chest was a long case made of satin-smooth metal. Alberic lifted it out and gazed at it for some time. 'I never did better work.'

'May I see?'

Alberic put the Great Canteen on the workbench. 'My captor locked it when I came to this benighted city and I don't have the key.' He gestured at the small, intricate padlock which was hanging from a clasp on the canteen. It was only the size of Nisha's thumbnail, but Alberic glared as if it were a poisonous snake.

Nisha blinked. 'If you can't open it, how do you know that it's missing a spoon?'

Alberic lifted the canteen with both hands. He closed his eyes. 'This canteen has five layers of velvet-lined slots. Each has nearly two hundred individual items. The slot in the top left-hand corner is empty and it is where the missing spoon belongs.' He opened his eyes. 'This canteen is part of me. I can feel that there is something missing.'

Nisha reached over and tapped the lock. 'It's tiny. If you don't have the key, why don't you cut it off?'

Alberic snorted. 'Impossible. It's made of yanlen.'

Chapter Eight

Fire & Metal

Nisha's face fell. 'Oh.' She knew of yanlen, a rare, extremely hard metal from one of the rift worlds. On one of her early morning excursions, she'd seen workers mending the gates near the Last and First Station with it. They had to fit ready-made bands into place as they couldn't shape it to fit at all.

'It can't be cut, bent, filed or crushed,' Alberic

said. 'I've spent five hundred years trying, with no success. Even if the Great Canteen was incomplete, I wanted to gaze on it again.'

Alberic put the case back on the bench. The lock jingled brightly and Nisha thought it almost sounded like laughter. 'Only extreme heat affects yanlen,' the old man said. 'It's said that yanlen will melt, if it is heated enough. But it will resist heat that would melt copper, or brass, or even iron. Yanlen can sit untouched in the heart of a blacksmith's forge.'

Nisha's mouth was suddenly dry. 'Heat? I might be able to ...'

Alberic blinked, and looked at Nisha. 'What is it you can do?'

Nisha took a deep breath. 'I have fire-magician heritage.'

At that moment, the floor underneath their feet swayed. Tools on the benches jiggled and rocked, and from the shop came the tinkling noise of hundreds of pieces of cutlery.

'Quentaris is uneasy,' Alberic said as he righted a fallen salt cellar. 'Five hundred years it's been and now I'm visited by a fire magician while the city trembles.' He put a finger to his lips and frowned.

'Tell me, what is the weather like upstairs?'

Nisha wondered why it mattered. 'It's hot. Very hot, and it's been so for weeks.'

This seemed to both trouble and delight Alberic. 'Well. I see. A streak of unusually hot weather, the city struck by tremors ... Strange times have come to Quentaris.' He tapped his lower lip with his finger. 'Come here. Let me look at you.'

Nisha came close to Alberic as he sat on the stool. His face was level with hers and he peered into her eyes, searching. 'Ah, the power is there all right. But it is unformed, rough around the edges. You need training?'

'I do. My parents died when I was young, before they had begun my instruction. But I'm learning. I think I can do something about that lock.'

'Great care would be needed,' Alberic said. 'You'd have to focus your fire on the hasp of the lock. If you lack control, the heat required could consume the whole Great Canteen. Indeed, it could devour this whole workshop.'

Nisha remembered the ravenous hunger of the fire she had unleashed on the Zolka and shivered. But even as she did, she recalled the feeling of the fire she summoned. It had thrilled her, but it had also filled her so full of power that she was in danger of losing herself to the flames and seeing all those around her as tiny, trivial creatures …

'Focus, concentration, control,' Alberic intoned.

Nisha closed her eyes and sought for her heart of fire. It sprang to life in an instant. She was determined to avoid the fumbling mistakes she had made with her power in the past, so she held grimly onto the surge that tried to overwhelm her. She held her power tightly, even as she stoked its fierceness.

'I have it,' Nisha breathed and she opened her eyes. Then, she held up her forefinger.

Alberic shielded his eyes from the light. 'Careful. Don't touch anything but the lock.'

Nisha was dimly aware of the brilliant white light that had flooded the workshop. The few remaining shadows were hard and black, and Alberic was squinting from between slitted fingers.

Nisha wasn't dazzled at all. She found the glare easy to look at as she strained to keep the heat from boiling out of her fingertip.

Carefully, she reached out and touched the hasp of the lock. The metal softened beneath her fingertip. Then it gave way with a puff of smoke and a sound like a sigh.

'Enough!' Alberic cried. He waved smoke away from his face. 'Stop before you burn the place down!'

Nisha drew on her strength. The fire in her fingertip seemed reluctant to depart, but she slowly quenched it.

Alberic sprang to a bucket near the hearth. 'Stand back,' he snapped, then he poured sand onto the workbench. The flames from the molten metal were smothered.

Dropping the bucket of sand, Alberic seized the Great Canteen. As soon as he had it in his hands, he smiled. 'No damage,' he said. 'You've been most skillful.'

With great care, he found a clear space on the workbench. When he lifted the lid of the Great Canteen, Nisha gasped.

After more than five hundred years, the knives, forks and spoons still glowed with a soft lustre. Slotted into place, nestled against each other, the delicate webwork of the handles made the Great Canteen look more like a tapestry than a collection of eating utensils.

But even as she was staring with wonder, Nisha's gaze was drawn to the single empty slot in the array. There, among the spoons, was the flaw in the perfect arrangement. It was like a missing tooth in a perfect smile or a crack in an intricate stained-glass window.

'Now,' Alberic said. 'To make the incomplete, complete.' Gently, he reached out and settled the missing spoon into place. He smiled and spread his hands. 'At last.'

Alberic closed the lid of the canteen and straightened. He was smiling, and Nisha thought that he was standing taller and looking stronger. 'There,' he said. 'You've done me a great service, Nisha.'

Nisha shrugged. 'The spoon was lost. I had to do my best to return it.'

'Ah, I understand.' Alberic bent and studied Nisha closely. 'I can see that your power is strong, but you still have much to learn.'

'I know,' Nisha said. 'I'm doing the best I can by myself.'

Alberic pursed his lips. 'There are old ways for helping young magicians who have no guidance. Let me think.'

With that, he crossed the workshop and stoked

the fire on the hearth. Nisha watched him anxiously. Could this strange man help her in her quest to master her fire-magician heritage?

'Fire,' Alberic murmured as he stared at the coals. Then he lifted his head. 'I remember now. It was a long time ago, but a powerful fire magician told me of a special amulet that was passed from fire magician to fire magician. It was a source of help and guidance for those who had none.'

'Who has it? Where can I find it?'

'The last I heard, it was in a sutler's store belonging to a friend of mine.'

'In Lower Quentaris?'

'Of course. And here's someone who can show you the way.'

Nisha turned towards the door. 'Damino! Where have you been?'

Alberic cocked an eyebrow at the boy, who was grinning in the open doorway. 'Damino, is it now?'

'Of course, Master Cutler! Damino, at your service!'

'Naturally,' Alberic said. 'Do your duty, then, and guide our friend to the sutler's store.'

'But where were you?' Nisha asked Damino.

The boy shrugged. 'I have others to look after. But I came back to you, didn't I?'

'He seems flighty,' Alberic said, 'but he is actually very staunch. He won't lead you astray.'

'Come, fire girl, let's be off. Mustn't dawdle!' Damino grinned and hurried off.

Chapter Nine

A Shop & a Soldier

THE journey from the cutler's shop to the sutler's store was swift. They encountered no crowds, only a few individuals. Almost all of them were muffled or masked, heads down as they hurried to whatever destinations called them. Nisha decided that 'mind your own business' was the motto of Lower Quentaris.

'We're right under the west wall of the city,' Damino said finally. 'The sutler's store is just ahead.'

Nisha looked up at the darkness above and thought for a moment. She tried to remember her journey so far. 'We're under the city barracks?' she asked Damino.

'Right you are! How'd you guess?'

'If I were a sutler, I'd set up close to where the soldiers were. It makes good sense.'

'Good sense! It's good to see that you're full of good sense!'

Damino skipped ahead, laughing. Nisha smiled at his antics, but at the same time she was convinced that the boy was more than he seemed. His cryptic asides and mysterious disappearances made him seem older than his years, but his caperings were carefree and child-like. He was a collection of pieces, Nisha thought, a mosaic put together from the fragments of many portraits.

'That's it,' Damino said, pointing at a long brick building. It merged with rock overhead, which pressed low in this part of the undertown. Two massive brick pillars stood to either side of the building, a landmark which Alberic Mallison had described. Behind one of the pillars, a stone staircase wound its way upwards.

Damino stopped outside the front door, hands on hips. 'Go in, see the sutler, tell her I brought you.'

'You're not coming in?' Nisha said.

Damino grinned. 'I'll run a ring around the city before you're done, I'll wager! Look for me!'

He immediately did a cartwheel, then raced away up the dimly lit street.

Nisha felt the walls of the undertown close by and the weight of the whole city pressing down on her from above. She shivered and, before her resolve melted, she pushed open the heavy door.

Inside, the sutler's store was long and narrow. Shelves lined each wall, from floor to ceiling. Trestle tables stretched along the middle of the room, towards the far-off counter, making two aisles either side. Lanterns spaced high on the shelves threw light that seemed tired and listless, bright enough to chase the shadows away but not enough to make a cheery scene.

Nisha paused on the threshold. The room was cool and dust made her wrinkle her nose. The air was stale and flat, and smelled of leather, rope and polish.

'It's old,' Nisha murmured to herself. It was like being in a room that had been shut up for years with no-one disturbing it, until only memories were left.

She swallowed and set off for the counter at the far end of the store.

Stepping lightly, Nisha took note of the neat arrangement of shelves. Each was stacked with the sorts of things soldiers might need but find hard to come across: good boots, polish, well-made saddle-bags, heavy cloaks, scarves, tasty items of foodstuff.

After the array of cutlery in Alberic Mallison's shop, Nisha's gaze was taken by the glittering display of knives. Racks and racks of them were laid out on the benches. Each handle was wired to the rack, to discourage theft. The smallest knife was the size of Nisha's little finger and she couldn't imagine it being useful for much more than peeling a pea. The largest was as big as her forearm, with deep grooves on its blade and a savage, upturned point.

Nisha wanted to linger, but the counter at the far end of the store drew her on.

'Boot scrapers,' she whispered, 'bottles of spirits, moustache wax …' All the bits and pieces to help make a soldier's life more bearable. No swords, shields or other weapons. She knew that the army supplied such essentials. The sutler was there to fill in the gaps, to provide what a soldier needed to keep going.

Nisha neared the counter. A small, red-haired woman was serving a soldier who was dressed in a tattered, muddy coat and boots. Water dripped from his clothes, but Nisha noticed that the floor beneath his feet was dry.

With a sweep, the sutler laid a row of cards on the counter. 'The Escardy deck is decorative,' she said to the soldier. 'Note the beauty of the Queen of Air. But it is not at all durable.' With one motion she swept the cards up and replaced them with another. 'For any prolonged campaign, you'll need the Tillerman deck.' She held up the King of Waves. 'The Tillerman deck won't fall apart if it gets wet, can be wiped clean of mud and is light enough to carry for leagues.'

The soldier tugged at his long, straggling moustache. 'The Tillerman it must be, then,' he said softly and Nisha shivered. The soldier's voice was dry and distant, more like a lost sigh than a voice.

Gold changed hands. The soldier leaned on the

counter and silently stared at the deck of cards. Then he picked them up and weighed them in one hand. 'I don't suppose I'll be back,' he said to the sutler. His gaze was somewhere above her head, as if the wall behind her had vanished and he could see his destination in the distance.

'No,' the sutler said gently. 'I don't suppose you will.'

The soldier shrugged, then turned and drifted past Nisha as if she wasn't there. Even though his boots squelched, he left no tracks as he went by.

Behind the counter, the sutler's gaze followed the soldier until he slipped through the doorway. 'Poor soul. So young and already lost.'

She rubbed her forehead wearily and then seemed to see Nisha for the first time. 'Oh,' she said and put a hand to her mouth. 'You're not dead too, are you?'

Chapter Ten

Goods & their Seller

IT took Nisha some time, but she finally managed to convince the sutler woman that she was alive and well.

'Alberic Mallison sent me,' Nisha said eventually. 'The cutler.'

'Ah!' she said. 'I see now. I thought you were one of the lost souls. Even though you look a little young to be a soldier …'

She lifted a hinged section of the counter and came to study Nisha. She was a small woman, barely taller than Nisha, and her hair was an elaborate array of curls and ringlets that reached her shoulders. 'Once, back in my native land,' she said, 'my establishment was so busy it was hard to find standing room. Troopers, guardsmen, officers, all came to my store to find the little things that made their life easier. And I could provide whatever they needed!' She drew herself up proudly. 'Tonic? Foot salve? Pimander tea? Of course! Sewing kit? Waterproof dressing? Dice that are fair and honest? Juleen's store was the place to come!'

Nisha looked around the store, now empty of customers. 'But not now?'

Juleen the sutler pushed her hair back with both hands. 'No. All has changed. All has changed since I've come to Quentaris.'

'The barracks are close by, aren't they?' Nisha asked. 'Business should be good.'

'No-one comes here. Only the dead.'

'But I saw someone. He bought a deck of cards.'

'He was lost some weeks ago, I'd say,' Juleen said.

'A border skirmish with Tolrush, from his stripes. They die so young.'

At that moment, Nisha felt a chill. The soldier they'd seen a moment ago was a ghost? That seemed to be what Juleen was suggesting. Nisha found it hard to believe. He was so solid, so real. But then she remembered how sodden he had been, how muddy and wet. How could this be when it hadn't rained in Quentaris for weeks?

Nisha had the feeling that she had left ordinary matters behind. The sunny, everyday life of the Old Tree Guesthouse seemed distant and almost unreal. Here, in Lower Quentaris, she was stepping into matters mysterious and — perhaps — dangerous. But she couldn't let go. The lure of the magical and the extraordinary called to her, and it was exciting.

Nisha cleared her throat. 'How long have you been here?'

'How long have I been selling small comforts to dead soldiers? How long have I been unable to bring cheer to the living?' Juleen held out both hands, palms upwards. 'As long as the cutler. Five hundred years, more or less.'

Nisha's mind reeled. Five hundred years of selling

provisions to ghosts? 'Just like Alberic Mallison,' she breathed. 'Are you bound to Lower Quentaris, too? Do you have something missing?'

'Oh yes.' The sutler looked searchingly at Nisha. 'Five hundred years it's been, and now the earth is shaking beneath us and the sun is blazing overhead. All the signs are in place. And it seems as if you are the one.'

'I beg your pardon?'

The sutler ignored her. 'Wait while I fetch something.'

Nisha watched as Juleen rummaged through shelves much taller than she was, pushing aside boxes, bottles, jars and bags. Shaking her head, she used a ladder on rollers to climb higher and continue her search.

The sutler mounted the ladder swiftly, dropping to the floor when she was dissatisfied with her search. She moved up and down like a kite in a fretful wind, plucking items from shelves and discarding them after a quick glance. Nisha wondered how the woman knew where anything was.

'Do you need some help?' Nisha called.

'No,' the sutler said from near the ceiling. 'I

hadn't thought about this for an age. But it is time for it now, I feel.'

Juleen descended the ladder carefully, using only one hand. The other cradled an object made of brass and wood. It was shaped like a box, but two tubes protruded upwards from it, one on either end.

'I brought this from Phrasis, my home,' Juleen said as she placed it on the counter. 'It's very old.'

Phrasis. Nisha remembered. 'That's where Alberic Mallison came from.'

'Of course. We were brought here together.'

'Brought here?' Nisha echoed. 'He said it happened against his will. And you, too?'

'Here. I'll show you, not tell you.'

Juleen gestured at the brass and wood box. 'One of the last things I did before being taken from Phrasis was to capture my memories in this device from one of your rift caves. Strange and powerful magic, it has. Look through the tube and you will see what happened to me — and the others.'

Nisha felt her heart start to pound. 'Is it like one of the new far-seeing devices?' she asked. 'The ones that allow the sages of the university to see the face of the moon clearly?'

Juleen raised an eyebrow. 'Somewhat. Put your eye to the tube. You will see.'

Nisha felt her stomach flutter, but leaned over the box and sought the eyepiece.

'Close your other eye,' Juleen said. 'And watch my story unfold.'

At first, Nisha saw nothing but darkness. Slowly, it began to clear. It was like peering through fog at midnight, but gradually she realised that she was looking *down* on a vast army, as if she were a bird. Tiny figures in armour, on horseback, brandishing weapons and banners, were laid out before her. She could hear nothing, so when weapons clashed, or horns were lifted, it was like a mime show. She gasped, then felt dizzy as the vision swooped and revealed that the army was arrayed in front of the walls of a city.

'Phrasis?' Nisha asked, without looking up from the eyepiece. She didn't think to wonder if Juleen knew what she was looking at.

'Yes,' she said. 'My home. Once it was fine and proud, a place of great learning. But a small group of sages fell into the way of darkness and took control of the city. Phrasis became a feared name, a threat to all.'

'Why didn't you leave?' Nisha asked. The vision below her showed that the walls of the city were broken in many places and the gates were shattered. Smoke rose from a hundred places inside the city.

'We were there before the city began,' Juleen said, 'we had no desire to leave. Even if the rulers were corrupt and wicked, the people were — at heart — still people. If we remained, the soul of the city remained — and its power.'

Nisha's gaze was suddenly taken by a tall figure on horseback, slowly emerging from the press of the army. Her armour was so bright that it made Nisha blink and in her hand she held a silver sword. With a start, Nisha knew that it was the legendary Queen Hermia, the warrior magician queen of long ago Quentaris.

The queen approached the ruined gates and six champions rode behind her. As she advanced, Nisha was suddenly brought closer. She could see the faces of the soldiers, cheering as she passed. They were banging weapons on shields, shaking fists triumphantly, proud of their leader. She smiled grimly as she came close to the gates, dark-haired and beautiful, and stopped on the threshold of the city.

Queen Hermia held up a hand, halting her champions. Nisha couldn't hear the argument, but the queen was firm, shaking her head. The champions were dismayed, even fearful, but remained outside the gates as the queen rode in alone.

'She was brave,' Juleen said softly. 'A powerful sage, with great magic at her command. Her only thought was to make Quentaris safe from the threat of Phrasis.'

Nisha was taken aback as the scene changed. Shadows were longer, even though the champions had not moved from their place outside the gates of Phrasis. Their faces were anxious, and there seemed to be much discussion and pointing towards the city.

At that moment, Queen Hermia emerged, her horse stepping carefully over the broken beams and rubble. Behind the queen came four figures. No chains bound them, but they were clearly held by the queen, following at her command.

Nisha peered at them. 'It's you!' she said, and lifted her head to stare at Juleen. 'And Alberic Mallison!' She wondered who the others were, but when she returned to the eyepiece, the box was dark. 'Oh! It's gone.'

She looked up and saw that Juleen was watching her carefully. 'I wanted to remember that,' she said, 'how we were taken to complete the ruin of Phrasis. After that, we were brought here to Quentaris so Phrasis would never rise again.'

'But you were bound here and kept harmless. How?'

'Come this way,' said Juleen.

Nisha followed the sutler as she swept out of the store. She stood on the pavement outside and pointed to a spot above the door. 'What do you see up there?'

'Nothing.'

'Exactly. Something is meant to be there.'

'A sign?' Nisha guessed.

'My special sign. I was set up in this store here, but my sign was taken away. It told everyone what I was and it was part of me. I will never be complete until I have it back. Only then can I restore myself and start selling to the living again.'

It was obvious what Juleen wanted. Nisha crossed her arms. 'Alberic Mallison told me of an amulet.'

Juleen looked shrewdly at Nisha. 'Wait,' she said.

'Did someone with gold and silver hair guide you to this place?'

'Damino,' Nisha said. 'A young boy. He helped me find the cutler's shop, too.'

'Ah. I understand now.' For the first time since Nisha had entered the store, the sutler smiled. 'You have fire-magician heritage, do you not?'

'Yes. But I haven't been trained.'

'Somewhere in my store is an amulet that could help you learn the control you seek.'

Nisha's hopes rose. 'Wonderful!' she said.

Juleen held up a hand. 'I cannot give it to you. Not until you do something for me.'

Of course. 'You want me to help you get your sign back.'

'Precisely.'

Chapter Eleven

A Sign & a Furnace

BEHIND the sutler's store was a vast yard, surrounded by a chest-high wooden fence. The lamplight here was uneven, but Nisha saw that the yard stretched into the black distance. Columns thrust up out of the yard like trees. When she looked over the fence, she saw a vast expanse of dimly lit rubbish.

Nisha turned to Juleen, but before she could say

anything the ground shifted and groaned, swaying like an overloaded beast of burden. A loud crash came from the near distance.

'More earth tremors,' Juleen said and looked up. 'Quentaris is uneasy.'

Nisha looked out over the heaps and mounds of broken boxes, fragments of stone, concrete and splintered beams. The yard was full of desolation and ruin.

Juleen swept an arm over the sight. 'If a new tunnel is carved out of the underground, or a collapse has to be cleared out, the rubble ends up here. If anyone desires, they can re-use this debris, but some of it has been here for centuries.'

Nisha frowned. She could feel something out there — something she couldn't see.

'I hope you can help me,' Juleen said. 'For Quentaris' sake.'

With that, she opened the gate and glided into the gloom.

Nisha grinned. She felt as if great events and high deeds were just around the corner. She set off after Juleen, hurrying before the shadows grew too thick.

As Nisha entered the wasteland, she felt something luring her, drawing her forward. Something was calling to her fire-magician heritage and her heart of fire was uneasy. She peered ahead and to either side as the path wound its way between the mounds of debris. Nisha stumbled over the uneven ground, keeping an eye on Juleen a few yards ahead.

Plunging through the half-light thrown by the few lanterns attached to pillars, Nisha felt, more than saw, her way. She held her hands up in front of her, palms outwards, as her skin began to tingle.

Before long, a faintly familiar smell tickled her nose, rising above the dust that lay heavily on the debris all around. Juleen began to slow and Nisha knew they had drawn close to their destination.

Not far away, Nisha could see a large bulky shape, looming as large as a building. It towered nearly to the rock above, black against the shadows. A few more yards, a final turn around a pile of broken statuary and Juleen emerged into a clearing free of any rubble. Immediately, Nisha was assaulted by heat.

'Oh,' she said as she stared upwards. 'A furnace.'

Nisha's gaze followed the huge chimney which disappeared into the shadowy rock overhead, and the piles of refuse around it.

'No,' Juleen said. 'It's an incinerator. To get rid of burnable rubbish.'

The incinerator was rounded, a gigantic iron barrel that reached high overhead. It had a door in the front as big as a tall man. It radiated heat, but Nisha felt it as a welcoming caress and trembled as she felt her heart of fire respond to the beating warmth.

'There's a chimney up there,' Juleen pointed. 'It comes up near the west wall of Quentaris, where no-one would notice another chimney among all the foundries and factories.' She eyed the metal monster suspiciously, as if it were an untrustworthy watch-dog. 'The incinerator has been here for hundreds of years, devouring almost everything thrown into it. Its fires well up from deep within the earth. The shape you see is simply an iron shell to keep it in one place, safe for us to use. Pipes run around it, and the result is torrents of hot water for Lower Quentaris.'

The heat from the incinerator beat on Nisha's face and hands. It tingled. 'It's a greedy beast,' she said.

'It is, but even with all its hunger, there are some things it can't consume.'

Pieces fell into place. 'Your sign is in there.'

'Indeed,' Juleen said, smiling. 'My sign was wrought by magic. Not fire magic, or any magic of the elemental kind. It was created through the magic of place and permanence, something that belongs to me. I endowed the sign with part of myself and my identity.'

'Which is why you want it back,' Nisha said.

'And you're the one to retrieve it for me,' Juleen said, 'from the heart of the fire.'

Chapter Twelve

An Inferno & a Rescue

THE challenge had been thrown down by Juleen, and Nisha's heart raced. But what about a more ordinary solution? 'Why can't you use a poker or something to drag it out?'

'We tried, but the heat melted it. We can see the sign in glimpses before the heat gets too fierce and we have to close the door. It is right in the middle of the inferno. But with your fire-magician power you should be able to resist the flames.'

The heat from the enormous incinerator now almost felt like a gentle patter of rain on her skin. She remembered the joy she felt when she drew on the power of fire to defeat the Zolka invasion and she wanted that feeling again. But then she recalled how she couldn't even control a small fireball in Stanas' cellar and how she had spoiled a whole vat of beer.

Could she do this? Could she trust her power?

'I can,' she said firmly.

Juleen squeezed her shoulder and stepped back. 'Please bring me my sign. And be careful.'

Nisha took a deep breath, and approached the incinerator.

As she drew nearer, the heat increased, but Nisha simply felt it as comfortable warmth. A core of fire rippled in the middle of her body and Nisha felt the warmth both inside and out. This, she knew, was her real power awakening. She began to breathe faster. Her skin started to tingle and it felt as if her blood was on fire.

Even her vision began to change. She began to see heat. Objects had shimmering outlines that pulsed and wavered. The mounds of rubble were dull — browns and blues, but she turned and looked at Juleen. Her outline was warm, living reds and oranges, and within it dwelt a small core of flame. Nisha waved, then turned back to the incinerator.

It was wreathed in a fiery outline, bright, searing yellow, almost white.

Nisha swallowed nervously and reached for the door of the incinerator. A pair of heavy iron tongs lay nearby, but she ignored them. If she needed tongs to open the door, there was no point going further.

The latch on the door was long and tarnished. As she stretched for it, she felt blazing heat. Then the heart of fire inside her flared a little and the latch was warm and comfortable in her hand.

The door swung back easily. Nisha gazed into the inferno while heat burst forth and flowed around her.

It was bright, as bright as the noonday sun, and Nisha blinked. Her hair and clothing flailed as air screamed around her, pulled into the furnace by the heat. Coals as large as her fist were strewn around the incinerator chamber, each one flaring with flames and sparks. But in the centre of the fire was a pool of what looked like liquid flame, so hot that it shone almost silver. In the middle of this pool was a dark, rectangular patch.

'The sign,' Nisha breathed and she gazed through the heat shimmer. How could anything survive in such a blaze?

Nisha rubbed her face a little and felt a grainy scratch where she must have trapped a spark. Wind rushed into the incinerator and her hair flew like spray on a stormy ocean.

Nisha leaned forward. The wild draft rushed past, then over the coals and up the immense chimney. She stretched out, trying to grasp the sign, but fell far short. There was nothing else for it. She had to climb into the incinerator.

Once she scrambled through the opening, she wondered why her clothes and boots weren't burning. If her power extended to protecting them, what else could it do? Could she protect others, share this strength with them? Putting this notion aside, she concentrated on crossing the shifting surface of the coals. Her clothes and hair whipped around in the updraught, and a vast chuffing noise came from all around as she carefully placed each step.

The further Nisha moved into the fire, the more the fire inside her sang. It leaped and writhed, making little bubbles of joy, and she found herself skipping over the coals. Even though she knew her peril, she almost laughed aloud.

When she neared the pool of fire, Nisha was glad to see that the sign was within reach. When she tugged, it skated easily across the surface of the liquid fire. She staggered backwards and almost fell onto the living coals.

The sign was a yard or so wide, and perhaps half that high, made of dark wood that was unfamiliar to Nisha. Two holes had been drilled in the top. Nisha guessed they were for screws or bolts, to allow it to hang from a rod over the pavement. It read 'Juleen Limnal, Sutler' in bold, black writing.

Nisha grappled with the sign until she had it in both hands. Then she carefully made her way back over the coals and flames, clambered through the doorway and left the fire. Apart from being a little sooty, she was completely untouched.

Nisha pushed the incinerator door closed with her shoulder and ran, clutching the sign, to where Juleen was clapping and cheering.

'Well done!' Juleen said. 'You truly do share the fire-magician heritage!'

'Here's your sign, Juleen,' Nisha said.

The small woman took it and bowed her head. 'When I made this sign, a long time ago, I invested much of myself in it.' She hugged the board to her chest. 'I am now complete again and I can feel my time is coming.'

Nisha felt her face grow warm, but this time it was not from the fire. In fact, her inner flame seemed to be settling down into glowing embers.

'Come,' Juleen said. 'I believe I have an amulet for you!'

Chapter Thirteen

Rhymes & Reasons

JULEEN took a small box from under the counter. She opened it and her face fell.

'What is it?' Nisha asked.

Juleen started to speak but simply shook her head and turned the box around.

Sitting on the velvet was a small round stone.

'I'm sorry,' Juleen said. 'I had no idea.'

Nisha stared at the stone. 'The amulet?'

'It's gone. I haven't looked inside this case for a long time. It could have vanished decades ago.'

'Or it could have happened yesterday,' Nisha murmured.

Juleen looked dismayed. 'I'm sorry, Nisha. I didn't intend to deceive you. This is not of my doing.' She gazed at the stone, studying it closely. 'But all is not lost.' She plucked the small stone from the velvet and then, with a quick movement, twisted it. It separated into two halves, but when she twisted them back together Nisha couldn't see the join at all. 'The amulet is with the mason. This is his stonework.'

'And this mason is another resident of Lower Quentaris?'

'Indeed. His workshop is on the southern edge of the undertown. If you tell him who you are, I'm sure he'll let you have it.'

Nisha touched the stone with a finger. 'I feel like I'm being swept away. Alberic Mallison's story and now yours, Juleen. I'm in the middle of a lost part of Quentaran history.'

Juleen smiled. 'An apt description, Nisha. This city is a strange and wonderful one, and its past is full of deeds heroic, dreadful and laughable. But one should always remember: history is like a river, one that stretches out to the dim past, sweeps through the present and flows to the future.' She squeezed Nisha's shoulder and Nisha felt the strength in the small woman's grip. 'You're part of the unfolding of something that began a long time ago. With your help, you may be able to bring it to a conclusion, helping Quentaris and yourself at the same time.'

Before Nisha left to find the mason's workshop, Juleen gave her a neat pack with provisions and a full water bottle. Nisha was immediately hungry, and opened a package of dried meat and tore off a chunk. 'This seems to say that the journey may take some time.'

Juleen looked guarded. 'It may. It may.'

'Is it possible, then, for you to get word to Arna, at the Old Tree Guesthouse? So she won't worry?'

'I'll find a way to get a message to her, be assured.'

Damino was waiting outside, leaning against a pillar, but he wasn't alone.

'Tal!' Nisha burst out. 'What are you doing here?'

Tal rubbed his hands together and looked embar-rassed. 'I came looking for you. I guessed you might be down here and that you could use some help.'

'But he got lost,' Damino crowed. 'I found him wandering around a nasty part of the undertown and brought him here. He's a lucky fellow.'

'I would've found you eventually,' Tal said. Then he smiled wryly. 'Not that I didn't appreciate the help, Damino.'

'My pleasure, drummer boy.'

Nisha wrinkled her brow. 'How did you know he was a drummer?'

'Look at his hands. Calluses on their heels. And see how he taps his fingers on his belt, beating out a rhythm.'

Tal dropped his hands and looked embarrassed again. 'Did you find Alberic Mallison?'

'Oh yes,' Nisha said. 'And I've found much more since.'

Tal was silent as Nisha described the mysteries of the cutler's shop, and he grew wide-eyed as she told him of the magical sign in the middle of the incinerator.

'I've heard of Queen Hermia,' Tal said when Nisha had finished. 'But bringing anyone back from Phrasis? I had no idea.'

'I think it's one of those details of history that's been lost over the years. Little pieces here and there have survived, but that's about all. Some memories linger long after the deeds have vanished.' As she spoke, something niggled at Nisha, but she couldn't grasp hold of it.

'What about the amulet, fire girl?' Damino asked, interrupting Nisha's thoughts.

'No amulet,' Nisha said. 'I have somewhere to go before I can find it.'

'Amulet?' Tal asked, and Nisha had to explain about her chance to find assistance in training her fire-magician skills.

Damino spread his hands wide. 'Never mind, never mind, we'll go across the undertown to meet the mason.'

Nisha blinked. 'I didn't say anything about a mason.'

'Your business is my business,' Damino said, and he shrugged. 'I hear things, and know other things.'

'Damino. I have to see the mason if I'm to find my fire-magician amulet, but there's more to this round-about quest than that, isn't there?'

Damino winked. 'True, fire girl. You've sensed it,

haven't you? There is always more to things than meets the eye, am I not right?'

'It's like watching a complicated dance, but not knowing the steps. I can see something is happening, but I'm not sure what it is.'

In counterpoint to her words, another tremor made the ground under their feet shiver. It rose a little, then settled with a sound like the grumbling of an unhappy banker.

'And we have to follow your lead?' Nisha said.

'*You* are leading. I'm helping. Cutler, sutler, mason ...'

'Cutler, sutler, mason,' Nisha repeated, and the phrase jogged at her memory. But she still couldn't grasp it. 'Tal, does that sound familiar to you?'

'Of course. You want to know any tune in Quentaris, just ask Tal. I never forget a song.'

'It's a song?'

'It's the old children's rhyme, Nisha.' He lifted his voice and sang.

One and two and three and four,
Queenie went off to the war.
Five and six and seven, eight,
Queenie came back through the gate.

'North and south and east and west,
Queenie laid them all to rest.
Round about and up and down,
Queenie bound them to the town.'

Nisha was puzzled. 'What do you mean, Tal? There's no mention of a cutler, or a sutler or anything.

'It's in the third verse. People mostly only sing the first two. But we musicians remember the rest.'

'Well, *I* didn't know there was more. Sing it for us, Tal.'

Tapping his foot, Tal sang:
'Cutler, sutler, mason, bard,
Watching, waiting is their guard.
Kept in place five hundred years,
Hostage to a city's fears.'

'Cutler, sutler, mason,' Nisha repeated. 'Tal, we're in the middle of a children's rhyme!'

'And what about in the first verse? "Bound them to the town." Isn't this rhyme telling the story of Queen Hermia and Phrasis?'

Damino beamed. 'You're doing well, you two. Go on, go on.'

Tal tapped his fingers on his chest. 'And what about the last verse, Nisha?'

'*But when the streets begin to bake,*
And the earth begins to shake,
Unless all are then set free,
Quentaris town shall cease to be.'

Nisha put a hand to her mouth. 'Oh Tal, do you think …?'

'Shaken to bits, Quentaris will be,' Damino said, 'unless you can set us free.'

Chapter Fourteen

Tremors & Perils

N ISHA felt as if she was beginning to see more. 'The old rhyme, Queen Hermia and Phrasis, the cutler, the sutler and the amulet, they're all part of the same puzzle,' she said slowly.

'And it seems as if there are two more pieces to complete,' Tal pointed out. 'The mason and the bard. Damino here says that Quentaris will be shaken apart if we can't help them.'

'That's it,' Damino said. 'Our time is short, so we must hurry.'

Nisha felt Damino's urgency and her curiosity made her eager to be off as well. 'Lead on, Damino,' she said.

'Gladly!'

Damino trotted off. Nisha had to walk quickly to keep up with him. The way, at first, was broad and well lit. Soon, however, they were forced to take narrower and more shadowy streets. Nisha saw how alert Tal became. He looked at each alleyway carefully as they passed, and he often glanced over his shoulder.

'Are you sure this is the way?' Nisha asked Damino.

'Of course! I'm never lost!'

Tal frowned, then looked up at the rock that was three or four yards above. 'We must be under the Square of Dreams. We're definitely heading south.'

Nisha looked up also and imagined the great buildings of Quentaris pressing down on them. Then she was taken aback when the rock above trembled. Spurts of dust puffed from on high, and gravel and sand sifted downwards. At the same time, the rock beneath their feet shook slightly and the lantern on the nearest column jiggled and flared.

'They're getting worse,' Tal said when the tremor had passed. 'Upstairs, the Archon has issued a proclamation telling us all not to worry. Naturally, that's made everyone suspicious.'

'Things will get much, much worse unless you can stop it,' Damino said. 'This way.' He pointed to a narrow gap between two shabby buildings.

Tal looked around nervously. 'I don't fancy the idea of being trapped down here in an earthquake.'

'Nor I.' She caught up with Damino. 'How can we prevent these tremors?'

'It's in the rhyme, fire girl! It's all in the rhyme!' Damino paused and looked ahead. The rock ceiling here was low, barely a yard above Nisha's head. The entrances to four laneways disappeared into the gloom ahead. A single lantern struggled to keep the shadows away. 'The one on the left!' Damino announced, and plunged into the darkness.

Nisha had to skip over mounds of refuse to catch Damino as he hurried down the laneway. She shuddered when her foot sank into something soft, but gamely kept her guide in sight. The walls close on either side and the low roof made the way seem like a tunnel. 'Damino!' she called. 'Wait!'

The boy turned and danced impatiently from foot to foot. 'We must hurry! There is much to do!'

Damino led them faster and faster, until Nisha was jogging through the mazy laneways. Tal kept close behind and she could hear his footsteps slapping against the stone pavement, but this was the loudest noise Nisha could hear. The undertown here was silent, and the houses, shops and buildings were dark. Even Damino seemed subdued as they hurried through the narrow lanes and alleys, with buildings huddled together as if frightened.

'Not far now,' he whispered as he helped Nisha and Tal through a gap in a fallen brick wall. 'At the end of this lane, on the right.'

The mason's establishment was a large stone building, but it, too, was dark and silent. 'No-one has been here for years,' Tal said, wiping dust from the front door.

'Wait,' Nisha said. 'There's a yard next door.' She looked around. 'Damino's gone.'

Tal stared into the gloom. 'I can't see him anywhere. Should I go and look for him?'

'No. He'll be back.' Nisha wandered over to the yard. It was stacked with blocks and slabs of stone. Broken fragments filled large barrels, and small, wheeled carts were laden with heavy blocks. Large hammers and metal bars were leaning against one of the stacks of stone, but they looked rusty and unused. Beyond the yard, in the guttering half-light, a large figure was labouring in front of a long stone wall.

He was a giant of a man. His shoulders were so broad that Nisha thought he'd have to turn sideways to go through most doorways. He wore a leather jerkin and heavy woollen trousers. He moved slowly and deliberately as he lifted an enormous block of stone over his head. 'Impossible,' Tal said from close behind Nisha. 'That stone is as big as a cow.'

The man lowered the block. It settled on the top layer of a wall made of other massive stones. He stood back for a moment, hands on hips. Then he adjusted the block until he was satisfied. After wiping sweat from his brow, he bent to another stone. With a single motion, he gripped it and raised it over his head. He shuffled a few steps before settling the stone next to its neighbour.

One hand on the small of his back, the huge man stood back and surveyed the wall. A single gap remained in it.

'We'll wait,' Nisha said. 'He's nearly finished.'

But even in the flickering light, Nisha could see that the mason's face wore no satisfaction. Instead, he looked afraid.

With sagging shoulders, the mason selected another huge block of stone. He picked it up easily and dropped it into place, completing the wall. But no sooner had the last stone settled than the whole wall heaved like a dying snake. Huge stone blocks tumbled like dice, crashing together with sharp thuds. Dust rose, splinters of stone flew, and with a roar the wall fell apart.

When the dust was quiet the mason was still standing there, unmoved. For a moment he was like a statue gazing over his ruined work. Then, slowly, he bent, seized a block and moved it back into place.

Nisha and Tal moved closer. The mason saw them and paused. 'Ah, I was wondering when you'd be along.'

'Please sir. I'm Nisha, and I'm learning to be a fire magician, and you ...'

'I know who you are and I know that you're after the amulet.' He cleared his throat with a grimace. 'I'm Gram Torbender, and I've been waiting a long time for you, I have.' The mason's voice was deep and throaty, as if he rarely used it.

'For me?' Nisha said.

'Aye. Once I felt the city shiver, I thought you might be coming along. Hot upstairs, is it?'

'It's the hottest summer anyone can remember,' Tal said.

'That'd be right,' Gram said slowly. 'Well, least-wise it might mean I can finish this wall, once and for all.'

'It was bad luck, it falling down like that,' Nisha said.

'Tweren't bad luck at all. It's always been that way. As soon's I get just about finished, it falls down and I'm bound to start again.'

'How long have you been working on it?' Tal said.

'Let me see now.' Gram's eyes went distant. His lips moved silently for a time, then he shook his head. 'I've lost track of time, I have.'

'The sutler and the cutler have been here for five hundred years,' Nisha said.

'Aye, we're all in this together,' Gram said. 'But I hadn't realised it had been so long. Our time is coming, I can feel it.' He squatted and placed one hand against the ground. 'Uneasy, down there, things coming to a head. If we can't get it sorted out, things will go badly for Quentaris.' He rose and dusted his hands together, then fixed his gaze on Nisha and Tal. 'You know about the rhyme by now, I expect.'

Nisha and Tal both nodded.

'It's all in there,' the mason continued. 'Your queenie, Hermia, was the prettiest queen I'd ever seen.' He smiled at the memory. 'You know, the only reason Quentaris defeated Phrasis is because Queen Hermia took us. Once we were gone, Phrasis soon became just a memory. Powerful she was, your queenie. But five hundred years is a long time for a binding spell.'

'So if her magic is growing weaker, you may be able to free yourselves?' Nisha asked.

'It's not as simple as that,' Gram said. 'Hermia made sure we were incomplete so that when she was gone we would be weakened, and still be bound to this place. But she wanted to be sure. She laid over us spells of great power and import. But when such spells run their time they can begin to unravel. Sometimes the frayed ends lash around and then ...'

At that moment, the earth beneath them rumbled and groaned. It shook briefly before quieting.

Tal nodded slowly. 'The tremors.'

'Aye,' Gram said. 'The tail end of Queen Hermia's spell. In her efforts to protect Quentaris so long ago, she could destroy Quentaris today. Unless we can be made whole.'

'What?' Nisha said. Her stomach was hollow. All she could think of was the towers of the city, the walls, the houses, all collapsing into dust. And the people ...

'If we're made complete,' the mason explained patiently, 'Queen Hermia's binding spell will have reached an honourable conclusion, instead of out-living its usefulness. It'll fade gently, most likely.'

'You're not human, are you?' Nisha suddenly asked, convinced that this was no ordinary man. 'What *are* you?'

Gram scratched his chin. 'It's hard to say, come to think of it. We'd been in Phrasis for an age or two, holding that city together, more or less. I suppose you could call us "powers". It's as good a name as any.'

'But someone who makes cutlery? Someone who sells things to soldiers?' Nisha said. 'I thought powers were meant to be more … more …'

'Grand?' The mason laughed quietly. 'Aye, that's what most people think. And in looking for the grand, they miss the power of everyday things. There's plenty of strength in a job well done, a service provided or a craft fulfilled.'

'I don't mean to offend,' Tal ventured, 'but that sounds like small magic to me.'

'It's strong magic,' Gram said. 'The magic of place and of simple craft.'

'Damino, too?' Tal asked.

Gram shifted uncomfortably. 'He's different,' he said eventually. 'He's not one of us, but he's part of all of us, in a manner of speaking. Helpful, but a bit flighty. As long as he visits each of us regularly, we keep him in order.'

'That explains his absences,' Nisha said.

'He doesn't look more than a child,' Tal said, grinning. 'But I'm learning that things aren't always what they seem.'

Nisha turned to the mason. 'Alberic Mallison had

his spoon taken away. With Juleen, it was her sign. And you're missing something, too?'

Gram rubbed his hands together. 'Aye, that I am. I can't make anything that'll stand without it. I'm bound to go on trying to make this wall, but my skill has soured. Every time I build this cursed wall, it falls. I can't do it without my plumb-bob.'

'Plumb-bob?' Nisha asked. 'What's that?'

'It's a mason's best friend, that's what it is. Without it, I can't make anything straight and true.' Gram reached out and picked up a fragment of stone. He held it up, blew on it, then picked at it with a fingernail.

'A plumb-bob is a weight, Nisha,' Tal explained. 'Made of lead, usually. It hangs from a line and gives you a vertical to work from.'

'Right you are, lad. You've done some masonry, then?'

'No. But I've watched stoneworkers around Quentaris. I play for them, sometimes, while they're working. They pay well.'

Gram smiled at that. 'I've been bound here to ply my craft, trying to build this wall, without my plumb-bob.' He sighed and took a small metal pick from a pouch on his belt. 'Fruitless, it is, but I'm bound to keep trying. I can't move from this yard until I'm done.'

Tal frowned. 'But can't you use another plumb-bob, or make one? Something small and heavy would serve.'

'Lad, Damino told me that you're a musician.' Tal nodded. 'Have you ever had to use someone else's drum and straight away felt uncomfortable with it?'

Tal nodded slowly. 'It didn't feel right. Everything I tried sounded wrong.'

'That's right. My plumb-bob fits me like my boots. I can't use another.' Gram blew on the stone in his hand, then rubbed it with his thumb. He took out a scraper from his pouch and frowned as he gouged at the stone. 'Find it and you'll help me. I'm sure I'll have found your amulet for you by then. I'll have it waiting for you when you get back.'

'Where do we find this plumb-bob?' Tal asked.

'Across that way,' Gram pointed with his scraper. 'Confined as I am to my yard, I've never been there. But I know that over there, where the streets end and the light begins to founder, Lower Quentaris gives way to shafts and tunnels older than the city itself. My plumb-bob is in one of them. Damino knows which one. Getting the plumb-bob back, though, will be harder than finding the shaft. Much harder.' The mason held out something to Nisha. 'Blow on this, and he'll come.'

Nisha put out her hand, and Gram dropped a stone whistle into it. It was eggshell thin and only the size of a copper coin, but Nisha could feel its strength as she took it between thumb and fore-finger. When she blew on the mouthpiece, the whistle let loose a wild wail that echoed off the rock overhead and vanished into the distance.

Nisha took the whistle from her mouth and stared at it. Gram had made it in minutes, yet it had such power!

'Hello!' came a familiar voice from the shadows. 'I'm here! Nisha, Tal, let's go! Time's a-wasting!'

Chapter Fifteen

Fog & a Descent

D AMINO hastened Nisha and Tal through narrow streets and tumbledown rows of houses. Even though another tremor rocked the earth while they were climbing over a mound of broken bricks, Damino beckoned them onwards. 'Hurry, hurry. Not far now.'

They eventually struggled through a laneway that was more like a tunnel than a thoroughfare.

'There!' Damino said when he emerged. 'The mason's precious plumb-bob is in that shaft!'

Laid out before them was a large open area, the largest Nisha had seen in Lower Quentaris, as big as the Square of the People in the city overhead. Dozens, hundreds of columns soared upwards, vanishing into darkness above, but so far apart that they looked like lonely trees on a windswept plain. Clusters of lanterns clung to the columns like strange fruit.

'Damino,' Nisha said as she gazed out over the shadowy expanse. 'What are all those holes?'

'Shafts,' Damino said, and he led them to the nearest. 'Old mines? The holes of strange underground beasts? No-one knows.'

'How deep are they?' Tal asked, but he stayed well back from the hole.

'Some are a few fathoms deep. Others seem to go down forever. There are all sorts.'

Nisha looked out over the shafts. Some were small enough to step over. Others were many yards across, and she wondered what they held.

Damino set off again, weaving a path through the shafts.

'Is that smoke?' Nisha asked as they skirted a shaft that she thought looked large enough to hide a regiment. 'That shaft over there?'

'Well spotted!' Damino said. 'Your eyes are sharp, fire girl! It's our destination, and I hope you're feeling strong.'

Smoke. Nisha shrugged. It seemed as if she was in for another test of her erratic heritage.

When they neared the shaft, Tal looked worried. 'Nisha, I don't think it's smoke at all.'

A white, roiling column issued from the shaft, disappearing high overhead. Nisha gingerly reached out. 'It's cold!' She tilted her head back to follow the billowing plume that rose upwards. Her hand was wet, and she wiped it on her jacket. 'I think it's fog, Tal.'

'Look, fire girl,' Damino said. 'Can you see the ramp? It spirals down, around the wall of the shaft. You'll find the plumb-bob at the bottom.'

The shaft was a stone's throw across and the column of fog rising from it was too dense to see through. Tal leaned forward, then straightened. 'The ramp starts right here, Nisha. It's wide enough.'

Nisha knew how much that comment cost Tal. He was never happy around heights. She peered through the fog. 'It's stone, the ramp.'

'Solid and stable,' Damino said. 'All the way to the bottom.' He rubbed his hands together. 'Go now, go now.'

Nisha chewed her lip, then looked at Tal. 'You can manage?'

He took a deep breath. 'Yes.'

Nisha led the way, and plunged into the fog, Tal close behind her. As the ramp slanted downwards, Nisha trailed her right hand along the wall of the shaft. The stone wall was slick and damp, and she soon found she was shivering. She sniffed. The air was dead and heavy, and smelled of mould and damp. Looking outwards, all she could see was the pearly-grey fog.

'Tal, are you cold?'

Tal's voice came from close behind her, muffled by the fog. 'Of course. It's freezing!'

Even though Nisha's fingers were numb from the rough stone, she could feel the cold rising from the shaft wall. The fog, too, ran its icy fingers on her skin and she shivered. She found she was thinking of ice and snow, Quentaris in winter, and her thoughts were growing sluggish.

Nisha dragged herself down the ramp, placing one plodding step in front of the last, slowly curling downwards through the blanket of fog. Muzzy-headed, it was all she could do to keep upright and not fall.

Suddenly, Nisha jolted and the woolly haze surrounding her mind lifted a little. A spark flared somewhere inside her, and she winced and looked around. The fog was still pressing close, but it was darker now, a forbidding grey. As she peered ahead, she felt the cold stealing in again, stealing her warmth and life.

Almost without realising it, Nisha fumbled inside herself and searched for, then found, her heart of fire. Gently, she roused it and quickly felt warmth running through her veins. Soon, her shivering had stopped and a few moments later, she realised that she was no longer walking downwards. Her footsteps crunched.

'Tal! We're here.' Nisha swung around. She held out her hands, searching for Tal through the fog. 'Tal?'

Chapter Sixteen

Cold & a Cure

Nisha told herself to stand still. She chewed her lip. She'd been sure that Tal was right behind her. What could have happened to him? With all directions looking the same, she didn't want to wander off and get lost. She carefully reached out with her foot, feeling around. She was relieved when she found the beginning of the ramp, leading upwards. 'Tal!' she called. 'I'm down here, on level ground!'

No answer. Carefully, she started up the ramp. With her left hand trailing along the wall, she realised that the wall felt gritty. When she brought her fingers close to her face she could see tiny ice crystals glinting in the dim light. She smiled, marvelling at how she still felt warm and snug even in such a frosty place, but then realised what the cold could have done to Tal.

Even while Nisha's anxiety grew, her foot caught on something. She stumbled and pitched forward.

For an aching instant, Nisha thought she was going to tumble off the edge of the ramp, but she rolled to her left and fetched up against the stone wall. A patter of ice crystals fell on her hair as she tried to regain her breath.

The huddled shape that had tripped her was nearby. She crawled. 'Tal!'

He was lying motionless. Hunched on his side in the middle of the ramp, his arms were wrapped around himself.

Nisha brought her face close to his. She could feel his shallow breathing, but his eyes were closed and his skin cold. 'Tal!' She shook him. 'Tal!'

The fog rolled around them and Nisha tried to sweep it away with her hand. 'Damino!' she called, but the fog caught her cry and swallowed it. She searched in her pocket for the whistle, but as soon as she put it to her lips, the thin stone shattered in the cold.

Nisha pressed her hands together and felt the warmth there — warmth that Tal needed. He was freezing to death while she was warm as toast. She had to find a way to share that warmth with him.

She roused the fire within her. She slowly called it up, struggling to keep it in check as it threatened to overwhelm her. Holding her fire tightly, she placed her hands on Tal's chest. She imagined a warm blanket, wrapping him entirely, making him cosy and comfortable. She pictured him enclosed in a bubble of summer air, relaxed and drowsy. She extended the warmth that enveloped and protected her until it included Tal as well.

'Nisha?' Tal's eyes opened, and he rubbed them with the back of his hand. 'Why am I so hot?'

Nisha sagged with relief. 'The cold had you. I'm sharing my fire.'

'Nisha.' Tal sat up and gripped her shoulder. His eyes were bright, his voice raspy. 'Nisha! I'm burning up! Stop it!'

'Tal!' Nisha took his hands in hers, then closed her eyes and clamped down on her fiery heart. It flared fitfully, but she didn't want it quenched completely. If that happened, they would both die.

'Tal!' She looked into his panicked eyes. 'I have to strike a balance! I must keep my fire alive enough to keep us warm, but not so hungry as to consume you!'

For a moment, Tal's grip was fierce. Then he nodded, and as he did, his grip relaxed. 'Ah, Nisha. That's better.' He let out a long breath and his eyes grew less bright, his skin less rosy. A moment later, he was standing and brushing himself off. Nisha studied him closely. His skin was pink and healthy, and he didn't look feverish at all. 'Are we nearly at the bottom?' he asked.

'It's not far,' Nisha said as she rose. 'You were nearly there.'

'Nearly,' Tal grumbled. 'I nearly froze to death.'

Nisha made Tal lead the way. She wanted to make sure she didn't lose him again and she kept a hand on his shoulder as they went. Soon, they had reached the end of the ramp.

The floor of the shaft was smooth, even and bare. Nisha and Tal crunched ice crystals with every step as they marched, arms linked, towards the centre of the shaft.

'I hate this fog,' Tal said, his breath steaming. 'How will we find our way back to the ramp?'

'We've left tracks.' Nisha pointed at the footprints in the ice crystals. 'It won't be hard.'

A dark shape loomed ahead. 'You think that's the plumb-bob?' Nisha asked as they drew near.

Tal nodded. It was a flat slab of rock, waist high, white and gleaming with ice crystals. He swept a hand, scattering them.

There, on the rock, was a dull silver tear the size of Nisha's palm. She took it and weighed it in her hand. Fat and heavy, it was as chill as ice — but Nisha's hand bloomed with heat and soon the metal was blood-warm. She looked through the hole in the narrow end, where a line would be strung. 'Yes. This is it.'

Chapter Seventeen

'**M**ASON!' Nisha called as they arrived at his yard. 'We have your plumb-bob!'

Gram was holding a massive block of stone in one hand and a hammer in the other. Two quick blows and he knocked the rough end off the block, leaving a clean edge. He dropped the block and waved.

Nisha and Tal hurried to him. 'We have it!' Nisha called, holding out the weight.

Gram thrust the hammer through a loop on his

belt and he scratched his chin. 'Aye, I thought you would.'

Nisha looked behind her. 'Tal, where's Damino?'

Tal looked around and shrugged. 'He led us back here from the shaft. I thought he was still with us.'

Gram snorted. 'Don't you worry about that one. He can take care of himself.' He held out his enormous hand. 'Now, can I have my bob?'

Nisha offered the weight. Gram folded his fingers around it. 'Ah.' He touched his chin, then his cheek, his eyes distant. 'That's better, that is.'

Tal tugged on Gram's sleeve. 'The amulet? Nisha's reward?'

Gram shook himself. 'Amulet? Ah, right you are.' He dug in the pocket of his leather apron. 'Here 'tis. Let's hope it's useful.'

He dropped it into Nisha's hand. She nodded and smiled wryly. 'Half an amulet.' She held it up. It was a metal semi-circle, with a fiery-red enamelled surface. It nestled in Nisha's palm, and was heavier than it looked. Although disappointed, Nisha had been half-expecting such a twist. Her journey so far had elements of a children's story, much as the children's rhyme had been their guide. To win the amulet before the story was over wouldn't have fitted.

Tal patted her on the shoulder. 'I'm sorry.'

Gram scratched his chin. 'Forgot that, I did. Half an amulet is about right. The bard has the other half. Find him and he'll make it complete.'

Nisha let out a long, slow breath. 'So we'll now go to meet the bard, to follow the old rhyme. "Cutler, sutler, mason, bard."' She rubbed the half-amulet with her thumbnail. 'And the bard will make the amulet complete.'

'True, lass.'

Cutler, sutler, mason, bard. 'The cutler is complete, now,' Nisha said. 'And so is the sutler, and you.'

'Just about, I'd say.'

'And when the bard is complete,' Tal said, 'all four of you will be made whole.'

'A complete set,' Nisha said, and the old rhyme came to her again. *Unless all are then set free, Quentaris town shall cease to be.* 'If you're all completed, you'll be set free? And the tremors will stop? Quentaris will be safe?'

Gram reached into his apron pocket and pulled

out a length of string. He strung the plumb-bob on the end and held it at arm's length. He closed one eye and studied the line. 'There'd be nothing to hold us here, if we were all complete. We've been bound for a long time. Once completed, we'll be unbound and we'll be off. If we aren't, the unravelling of Queen Hermia's binding spell will make the earth shake enough to ruin the city.'

Nisha felt the weight of responsibility on her like a set of uncomfortable clothes. 'We'd best be off, Tal.'

After getting rough directions, Nisha and Tal made their farewells to the mason and left him squaring blocks of stone and sighting down his plumb-bob.

Nisha wasn't surprised when Damino joined them before too long. 'The bard?' he asked as he skipped alongside them. 'I know where he is.'

Nisha peered along the empty street. 'The mason told us where to find him.'

'Pish! Gram Torbender hasn't left his yard in five hundred years! What would he know?'

Tal grinned. 'Lead on, Damino. Let's help Nisha see this thing through!'

Suddenly, Nisha was thrown off her feet. She landed heavily on her side, then rolled to her stomach. Dazed, she heard a deep-throated growl coming from underfoot, and the sound of cracking timber and stone. The cobblestones underneath fell rapidly, then rose just as quickly, catching Nisha squarely in the midriff. All the air was driven from her lungs. She gasped and scrabbled for a handhold as the road bucked and rolled beneath her. Dust stung her eyes and the rumbling went on and on.

Gradually, the ground calmed. Nisha lay there, eyes closed. She was able to breathe again, and she enjoyed the simple pleasure.

'Nisha, it's all right.'

Nisha opened her eyes to see Tal offering a hand. 'I was winded,' she explained as he helped her up. She checked in her pocket, and felt the shape of the amulet.

'That's the biggest tremor we've had,' Tal said. He wiped dust from his face.

Damino seemed quite untouched, but Nisha saw how worried he looked. 'This way.'

Damino took them through more populated areas of Lower Quentaris. The streets were full of tiny but thriving shops and stores, a compact market, a large cooper's workshop with the barrel-makers steaming and bending staves with gusto.

'Why would anyone live here?' Nisha asked as they hurried past a row of tiny, box-like houses.

'Habit, tradition,' Tal said. 'Families have roots in this place.'

'Besides,' Damino said, before urging them up an alleyway strewn with broken crockery, 'it's cheaper than the overtown. A place in the sun costs money!'

'Where are we?' Nisha asked. 'What is above us in the overtown?'

Damino grinned.

Tal frowned and looked up at the dim rock above. 'East wall?'

'Right, drummer boy! We've covered the city. The cutler, the sutler, the mason and the bard are at the points of the compass, ringing Quentaris.'

'*North and south and east and west,*' Nisha recited, '*Queenie laid them all to rest.*'

Chapter Eighteen

Whole & Complete

Nisha pushed past a young couple who were solemnly looking through the window of a tiny pastrymaker's shop. Tal strode alongside her.

'We're near!' Damino said, and he pointed at an open doorway.

Damino pounded up a flight of stairs, disappearing into darkness. Nisha shuddered when she saw a rat gorging itself on one of the mounds of refuse on the landing. Tal's face was grim as they passed doors from behind which came cries, shouting and — once — soft sobbing.

Four flights of stairs and they had reached the top of the building. 'No-one lives up here, this close to the overtown,' Damino said as he passed doors which looked as if they had been boarded up long ago. 'Except one.'

Nisha could see right through the holes in the wall at the end of the corridor. She realised that this was the tallest building she'd seen in the undertown, four whole storeys.

Damino stood by the only door which wasn't boarded up. 'The bard is here.'

'You'll wait outside, of course,' Tal said.

'Watching, waiting, I'll keep guard,' Damino said slyly.

Nisha heard the old rhyme in his words, but before she could say anything, Tal turned to her. 'Nisha?'

'Knock first.'

Tal rapped on the grimy door, then wiped his hand on his shirt. The door swung open a little.

'Go away!' a voice screeched. 'Leave me alone!'

Nisha glanced at Damino. 'A rather unmusical bard.'

Damino shrugged. 'His time has been hard.'

Tal put his mouth close to the door. 'Excuse us!' he called, 'but we have to see you! We may be able to help!' He pushed the door, but it refused to open. 'Locked. What should we do now?'

As she tried to rub the weariness from her forehead, Nisha considered their actions. She could call on her fire-magician power and burn the lock out of the door, but that wasn't likely to create a good impression. They needed a way to soothe the anger she heard in his voice, a way to appeal to him …

'Tal, he's a bard. If he hears music, he may let us in.'

Tal looked sheepish and reached into the pouch at his belt. 'I didn't bring my drum. All I have is these finger-cymbals.'

Brass-bright and shiny, even in the dim light, the four finger-cymbals were tiny, barely covering Tal's fingertips. 'It's all we have,' Nisha said. 'See what you can do, Tal, please.'

While Nisha and Damino watched, Tal fiddled with the finger-cymbals, adjusting them until he was happy. 'I wish I had my drum,' he said.

'Play, Tal,' Nisha urged. 'Open the door with music.'

Tal nodded decisively, then stepped up to the door. With a flourish, he snapped his fingers together. A clear, cheerful ringing jumped into the air and it was soon followed by another, then another. The rhythm of the finger-cymbals began slowly, but Tal lifted his hands and the chiming, bell-like sounds began to weave together in an intricate pattern.

Nisha smiled. She'd always loved the carefree joy with which Tal took to music. He gave every tune all his effort and his heart was in every piece of music he made.

Tal's brow began to sweat as the ringing of the finger-cymbals took flight. The music was methodical, with a strong, repetitive beat, but throughout it Tal would veer in unexpected directions, helping the pattern build and grow like a jungle, lavish and abundant.

Nisha caught Tal's eye and he nodded. He caught the rhythm, held it, and eased it to a finish.

The door opened.

Tal stood back and let Nisha enter. Tal followed and Nisha's eyes widened when she saw what the room held.

Dozens of candles were perched on shelves right around the room. The soft light was reflected from the host of musical instruments hanging from the high ceiling.

Tal gaped. Nisha watched as his hand slowly reached upwards, almost of its own accord. He pulled it back just as he was about to touch an ornately-patterned drum. Or was he looking at that golden harp, the one with strings like blue ice?

Nisha's gaze lingered on brass horns dangling like stalactites and a family of recorders ranging from a baby the size of her finger to a grandfather as long as her arm.

'Tal. What is this?'

'Viols,' he said. 'Oboes, I think, too. And mandolins, rebecs and flutes. And others I've never seen before.'

'They can stay up there,' a voice spat from the corner of the room. 'They can hang, for all I care.'

Nisha turned to see a spindly figure hunched in a chair. The man's long, pointed nose curved towards his chin, and his hair was grey and wild. He glared at them with wild, mad eyes. Nisha had seen eyes like that once before, when a travelling tinker arrived at the Old Tree Guesthouse with a caged falcon. The bird had been in the cage for a whole year, the tinker had explained, and would savage any hand that came close. Nisha had never forgotten its red-rimmed eyes and fierce stare. 'You play all of these instruments?' she asked the man.

'Not any more,' he said. 'Now my music's gone, I'm no-one.'

'What's your name?' Tal said.

'With my music gone, one name is as good as another.' He paused, and his shadowy figure straightened. 'I have been called Cam, long, long, ago. It will do.'

Nisha closed her eyes and bowed her head for a moment. She could see that this task was going to be harder than the others. She could return a spoon, find a sign, restore a plumb-bob to its owner. But how do you restore music to someone who has lost it?

'You've been here for five hundred years, haven't you?' Nisha asked. 'Like the cutler, the sutler and the mason?'

Cam narrowed his eyes. 'Oh yes, five hundred years.' Then he rose, glancing coldly at the array of instruments hanging from the ceiling. Light shone on the instruments, glowing on frets, valves and strings, ruddy polished wood and warm brass. 'I was brought here, with the others, and bound to this place. We were forced to stay, captured as spoils of war. And every day has been torture.'

Nisha was confused. The others had seemed sad, not angry like Cam. 'Are you in pain?' she asked.

Cam threw up his hands and scowled at the ceiling. 'It was easy for the others.' Slowly, he formed a fist and rapped it against the wall. 'What did they have to lose? Nothing important.'

'It seemed important to them,' Tal said.

Cam snorted. 'Making cutlery and stone walls. Selling little things to little people. Nothing compared to what I lost.' He flung out an arm and took in the collection of musical instruments suspended in the light and shadows. 'Once, I could play all of these. I created music to make you weep one minute and dance the next. I sang songs that made animals stop and listen.' He glanced at Tal. 'You, boy. You've been touched by music, haven't you? I heard it through the door and it was the only reason you were able to enter.'

'It was me.'

'What is it like when you're playing and the spirit takes you? When the music makes you soar like an eagle? When your soul is a hundred times larger than it usually is? When perfection floats around and you can touch it?'

Tal let out a deep breath. 'That's it. Just as you've described. When I'm drumming, sometimes, the music takes me away and I fly.'

Nisha put her hand in her pocket and felt the amulet. Its warmth encouraged her to press on. 'You've lost all this?' she said to the bard.

Cam clenched his fist and closed his eyes. When he opened them again, his fierce gaze touched Tal, then Nisha. 'I was brought here!' he snapped. 'By your queen! She won her war, took me away, and then left me here without my music, stranding me in this place! Look!' He stabbed a finger at what Nisha thought were three life-sized statues against the wall. 'Look at my treasures! Just before your queen took me, I gave them some of my music and since landing in this benighted city, they're cold and gone. My music is gone with them.'

Cam tilted the lantern. Nisha moved over and studied the three wooden figures.

Initially, she thought they were colourful statues. The three women stood in a cabinet which came up to their waists. One had long red hair, the other dark curls and the third had short-cropped hair that was almost white. All wore uniforms with bold displays of gold braid, blue serge and red silk.

Cam noticed her puzzled frown. With a sneer, he leaned over and opened the doors to the cabinet.

Nisha gasped. 'They have no legs.' She touched a wooden arm. So these were simply torsos. But why? She moved the jointed arm of the nearest statue. 'Puppets?' she asked Cam. 'Dolls?'

'Automata,' he corrected. 'Clockwork, gears and levers, and yet they could play any musical instrument known. I made them to accompany me and we were going to be the most perfect ensemble in history. I would sing and they would complement me. Or I would play an instrument of my choice and they would provide the accompaniment against which I would shine.'

Cam smacked his fist into an open palm. 'I

breathed my musical soul into them, but the spark was taken from them. They are dead.'

Tal looked at Nisha. 'They remind me of Jarmat Baldish. And it was a fire magician who animated that puppet.'

Nisha nodded. Only a few months ago, just before the Zolka invasion, both she and Tal had seen a similar creation. This had been animated by a Bruntian fire magician to make mischief in Quentaris. When active, it was almost human.

Tal put a hand on Nisha's shoulder. 'You can do it, Nisha. You can use your heritage to bring these dolls back.'

'Not dolls,' Cam flared. 'Never dolls. Could dolls make such music that the nightingales stopped singing so they could listen? Dolls? Bah!'

Nisha thought deeply. Could she? The Bruntian fire magician had been a fully-grown woman, and no doubt had been well-trained. The effort to animate the Jarmat Baldish puppet had been such a strain on her that she had almost collapsed …

Cam took a deep breath and passed a hand over his face. 'But perhaps you're the fire magician we've been waiting for. The time is right, after all.' He steepled his fingers together. 'Interesting. Did you know your Queen Hermia was a fire magician?'

'The one who put you here?' Nisha said. 'I didn't know that.'

'Think,' Cam said. 'You say you've met the cutler, the sutler and the mason. Did their incompleteness have anything to do with fire magic?

Nisha saw what he meant. She needed her fire magic to open the Great Canteen so Alberic Mallison's spoon could fit back into place. The recovery of the sutler's sign needed a fire magician, there was no doubt about that. The plumb-bob? She smiled. Who else but a fire magician could have fought off that cold?

'My music is still in the automata,' Cam said, his wild gaze softening. 'Their animation has been quenched. If you can restore that, they will be able to play. And I will be complete.'

'You can do it, Nisha,' Tal urged. 'If he's complete, the old rhyme will be complete. And the earthquakes should stop.'

Nisha took a deep breath and gripped the amulet in her pocket. 'I can try.'

Cam's gaze was on her as she studied the three

automata. She saw the hinges at shoulder and elbow, and the tiny joints in the fingers. The fingers themselves were long and tapering and the hands were resting, palm down, on the wooden cabinet top.

Nisha remembered the Bruntian fire magician. She had summoned white flame, then forced the puppet to breathe in the fire.

Concentrating, she felt for her heart of fire, then woke it gently. She knew that this was a task that required fine control. It wasn't a raw flaring of power. That would be too much for the automata. She had to use fire to create, not destroy.

Nisha held out her hand and spread her fingers. A ball of fire appeared, pulsing red and orange. She covered it with her other hand. The ball stopped pulsing and changed colour. Soon, it was brilliant white, and all shadows vanished from the room.

'Are you sure that's right?' Tal said.

Nisha glanced at him and saw that he was shielding his eyes. 'I don't know,' she said. 'It's the best I can do.'

She held the glowing ball under the nose of the nearest figure, sweeping the red hair back from its face as the fire came close. The ball of fire seemed to waver and hesitate before it slowly shrank, rose and disappeared up the wooden nostrils.

The automaton jerked, its joints clattering, red hair flying. Nisha jumped back. The bard's creation was quivering upright and Nisha was sure that if it had had eyelids, they would have snapped wide open.

'Quickly!' Cam said. 'See to the others!'

As Nisha attended to the next doll, the bard hobbled through the dangling instruments. 'You, boy!' he called to Tal over his shoulder. 'Find the best three-coiled horn! Be quick about it!'

Nisha concentrated on summoning the animating fire. When the second automaton twitched and flung its arms wide, she took a step back to avoid the flailing arms. It shuddered violently, and all the hinges and joints creaked before it settled.

By the time Nisha had awoken the third automaton, Cam was thrusting a silver flute into the hands of the first. Although its face was unmoving, the automaton seized the flute hungrily.

The old bard snatched the three-coiled horn from Tal and gave it to the second automaton. He then picked up viol and bow, and Nisha saw Tal stare at it.

'It's beautiful,' he whispered to her.

'Ah,' the old bard said softly as he gave the viol to the third automaton. His shoulders sagged for a moment, but when he straightened, Nisha thought he looked stronger — and even younger. 'I had almost forgotten what it was like.' He stepped back, hands on hips, and smiled at his happy trio.

All three looked alert and ready. The horn player and the flautist had instruments to their lips. The viol player had her chin on the rest and the bow ready. All three were trembling, alert.

Cam rubbed his forehead. 'I haven't seen the others for a long time. The mason, the sutler, the cutler. If it hadn't been for our messenger, I would have been alone with my madness and loss.' Even though his words were for Nisha and Tal, his gaze was on his trio. 'He needs to come to each of us, you know, or he begins to lose his substance.'

Tal blinked. 'Are you talking about Damino?'

'Damino? The golden-haired one?' Cam said. For a moment, he looked puzzled. Then his expression cleared. 'Yes, that is one of his names. He's part of us. We cannot leave the undertown, but he can go forth for us. He has been exploring, and watching over us for years.' He reached out and touched the first automaton, stroking its long red hair. 'He found where the cutler's spoon was, not long ago. And he told me of the trials of the others, how they struggled with being incomplete. But it gave me no comfort to know that others suffered, because I knew my suffering was greater.'

'They kept working,' Nisha pointed out. 'They tried to deal with their loss.'

'Their loss? Hah!' The bard snapped his fingers. 'Their loss was nothing, compared to mine. I lost my music!'

The old man's selfishness made Nisha narrow her eyes. 'Well, you have it back now, don't you?'

This made Cam stop short. 'I'm not sure.'

'Try,' Tal suggested.

The bard licked his lips nervously. Then turned away and wandered among the musical instruments for a while. Nisha could hear him humming. It was a soft, hesitant noise, and Nisha wondered if Cam realised he was making it.

A minute later, Cam returned with a tiny harp. It was barely larger than his long hands. He smiled crookedly at Nisha and Tal. 'One of my favourites.

At least, at home in Phrasis it was.'

Tal moved away from the automata and joined Nisha. They watched silently as Cam touched each of the wooden figures, adjusting joints and checking movements. Finally, he appeared ready. He stood tall, fingering the frame of the harp. Nisha watched as fear, loss and hope lingered on his face. Then he struck the strings.

The dry, still air in the room was suddenly full of wonder. For Nisha it was as if a swarm of golden insects had suddenly appeared, bringing light and movement to the world. She smiled, and saw that Cam the bard was smiling as well.

Shimmering notes rolled from the harp and it took Nisha some time to realise that the three automata were playing along with Cam. So fine was their accompaniment that it melded and supported the bard's harp-work, hardly seeming to be there at all.

Nisha realised that she was listening harder than she had ever listened before, but it seemed no effort at all. She became aware that Tal was by her side and he had found a drum. He was using both hands to create an intricate rhythm that swooped and danced around the melody before becoming a subtle, elusive beat. It added to the music in the room, never intruding, always welcome, like the perfect guest.

Suddenly, the bard placed his palm on the strings of the harp and all the music vanished. Nisha put a hand to her chest and felt her heart beating, and wondered at the glory of what she had just heard.

'I have it,' the bard breathed softly. 'My music has come back.'

Then, without warning, he softly began singing familiar words.

'One and two and three and four, Queenie went off to the war …'

Nisha's eyes grew wide as she listened. Somehow, Cam was taking the old children's song and turning it into a lament, accompanied by his magical trio. He sang the childish words and gave them a sense of loss that made Nisha's breath catch in her throat. The melody was no longer that of skipping and chanting children. Now it was a solemn unrolling of ancient history.

Nisha heard a choked sob by her shoulder and she realised Tal was taken up in the unfolding sadness. She felt tears in her eyes. The bard and his animated accompanists shared with them the injustice of being taken from their home and of being held, incomplete, for five centuries.

The bard and his trio came to the end of the song, and they let the music fade away. Nisha wiped her tears with the back of her hand. 'I'm sorry.'

'As am I,' Tal added. His voice caught in his throat, and he took a moment before he went on. 'We shouldn't have stolen you as we did.'

The bard was silent. Gently, he placed his harp on the cabinet, next to the silver-haired automaton. 'It was long ago,' he finally said without looking at Nisha and Tal. 'Phrasis had done terrible things to Quentaris. Your queen did what she felt best.'

'It may have ended the war, but it was still wrong,' Nisha said.

'Can you go home to Phrasis now?' Tal asked.

Nisha jumped when a voice came from the doorway. 'We can go home, but not to Phrasis, drummer boy. We are made whole, but nothing can bring back Phrasis.'

'Damino!' Nisha said, but she saw that their guide wasn't alone. Three figures followed him through the doorway. The sutler was first, holding her special sign in front of her like a shield. The cutler was close behind and he had his Great Canteen under one arm. The mason stooped and ducked his head under the lintel, then waved to Nisha and Tal. When he saw Nisha's quizzical look, he patted the pouch at his belt and smiled.

Damino skipped to where Nisha and Tal were standing. 'Done, I'm all done. See? I've brought them all together!'

'He's right,' Alberic Mallison said. 'In a manner of speaking. It might be more correct, of course, to say that we brought ourselves together. With your help, Nisha, naturally.'

Solemnly, all four bowed to Nisha in thanks for her part in their release.

Juleen raised her hand. 'Cam,' she said, her voice warm and tender. 'It's been too long.'

The bard nodded. 'Juleen. Alberic. Gram.' He crossed the room and stood facing them. The cutler, the sutler and the mason studied the bard closely for a moment. Then, as one, they held out their magic items — the Great Canteen, the sign, the plumb-bob.

Nisha gasped as the special objects disappeared.

'The musical trio,' Tal said. 'It's gone too!'

The cutler, the sutler, the mason and the bard stood tall. They smiled, nodded, and linked arms in a tight circle.

'Damino!' the mason called. 'Here!'

Damino shrugged at Nisha and Tal. 'I'm nothing without them.' He slid under their linked arms and popped up in the middle of the circle.

Immediately, the five figures shone with a ruddy light and the room came alive with sounds and smells. Nisha heard voices rising, bargaining good-naturedly, and the clink of cutlery on fine china. She heard coins jingling, soldiers singing marching tunes and delicate stringed instruments making lullabies for the sleepy. She jumped when Tal sneezed beside her.

'Stone dust,' he said. 'And was that boot polish I smelled? Or was it valve oil and resin?'

In the middle of the circle, Damino was laughing, a silver and golden figure. He danced a small jig and suddenly he vanished. In his place stood a tall figure with a gold and silver forked beard.

Tal gasped and tugged Nisha's arm. 'It's the stranger who told me I'd find something in the rift caves to help you! He and Damino were one and the same!'

The figure winked and waved to Nisha and Tal. A soft flare of light and he was gone.

The remaining four broke the circle and stood back. 'We are whole and complete again,' the mason rumbled, and Nisha heard how his voice had changed. When she met him in his yard, his voice was weary and tired. But now, his voice was full of patience, care and strength. Nisha knew that this voice belonged to someone who would measure carefully before cutting, someone who would spend an age building good foundations before moving upwards.

Nisha looked at the four. All were smiling, stealing glances at each other as if they couldn't quite believe they were back together. They had all changed. Light played on their features and ran across their bodies. They stood tall and proud, and Nisha decided that they were more solid-looking. Juleen the sutler had her hands clasped tightly, and her eyes were bright. Alberic Mallison still looked old, but it was the sort of age that suggested he could simply go on and on forever. The mason's back was straight, as if an enormous load had lifted from it. He seemed barely able to stop himself from grinning.

Resentment and frustration were gone from the bard's face. He smiled gently and the smile sat easily on his face.

'Damino's gone?' Tal said.

'No,' Juleen said. 'He is part of us, as he always was. We created him through our craft, to do the things we couldn't. He took a little from each of us and that was his strength. Now his job is done, we've taken back what we gave.'

'But who knows?' Cam said. 'We may need him again some time, where we're going.'

'What's your destination?' Nisha asked. 'Not Phrasis?'

'Phrasis is long gone, buried under the shifting sands of the desert,' said Alberic.

Juleen smiled and squeezed Nisha's elbow. 'That doesn't matter,' she said. 'We'll find somewhere to rest.'

'Somewhere far away, I think,' Alberic said. He flexed his fingers and rubbed his hands together. 'We can set ourselves up discreetly and practise our crafts.'

'We may try the rift caves,' the mason rumbled. 'A thousand worlds lie there. Plenty to choose from.'

Cam laughed. Nisha was glad to hear that the laugh was full and wholesome, without the bitterness the bard had previously worn like a suit of armour. 'Fortunately,' he said, 'we have plenty of time to explore them!'

Nisha frowned. It had been a frantic day. She'd been in a furnace, saved Tal from freezing, and brought puppets to life. 'I've learned a great deal about my fire-magician heritage,' she said to the four. 'But what about the amulet? I still need the other half.'

The bard put a finger to his lips in thought. Then he crossed the room to a small, lacquered cabinet. 'Here!'

He flung a glittering shape across the room to Nisha, but Tal caught it in one hand. 'Nisha,' he said, 'do you have the other half?'

She fumbled in her pocket for the half-amulet. For a moment, she thought she'd lost it, but then her fingers found the rough edge.

'Here,' she said, and Tal gave her the second half.

When Nisha brought the two pieces together, she felt them fit perfectly. As long as she held them together, the amulet didn't fall apart. It was whole, but she wondered how it would help with her fire-magician heritage.

Even as she wondered, the answer came to her. 'It's a keepsake, isn't it?' she said to Juleen. 'Having it isn't as important as the journey to find it. Am I right?'

'Of course,' Juleen said. 'But it is useful in its own right. It may not have any knowledge of its own, but it will help you remember what you've learned. The way you used your heritage to bring us together, that was the important thing. We waited five hundred years for Queen Hermia's spell to wane. But we knew we still needed help from someone who belonged to Quentaris itself. Nisha, your part in this final chapter was vital.'

'It was?'

'Aye,' the mason said. 'You're part of this city, and you're part of its history going back to Queen Hermia and beyond. Your efforts in freeing us helped to right the wrong which had been wrought on us. It was like the city was saying sorry, with your help.'

'True,' Cam said. 'Without you, we couldn't have prevented the backlash from Hermia's spell as it decayed.'

Nisha's face felt warm, but she knew it wasn't her fire magic flaring this time. 'Oh,' was all she managed to say and she stared at the amulet in her hand.

As if in an orderly dance, the cutler, the sutler, the mason and the bard took up places facing each other. Smiling, they clasped each other's hands.

'Wait!' Tal said. 'What about the earthquakes? Is Quentaris safe?'

'Of course! Trust the old rhyme!' Alberic said.

A burst of ruddy light and they were gone.

Tal and Nisha were alone in the room. 'We're safe,' she said to Tal. 'It's over.'

It was Tal who led them out of the bard's dingy quarters. Nisha clutched her amulet and was silent as they wound their way through the streets of the undertown. She studied it as Tal paused at crossroads and guided her along laneways. The amulet was warm to her touch and she knew that long ago it had been made with fire magic. The seam where the two pieces met was uneven and bumpy.

At the foot of a stone stairway, she gathered her fire magic. She brought heat to her fingertip and smoothed out the rough seam. Soon, the two halves were wedded with a thin, almost invisible, crack.

Tal waited, then led her up the steps. 'Almost there, Nisha.'

'What's that noise?' She looked to where Quentaris lay waiting.

Tal stopped, frowning. 'I'm not sure. Hissing?'

Nisha cocked her head and listened intently. It wasn't just a hissing noise — shouts and cries floated down from the city above. And a smell, a familiar, distant smell …

'I know what it is,' she said, grinning, and raced up the stairs, taking them two at a time.

'What is it?' Tal said as he hurried after her. 'Nisha! What is it?'

Then she scrambled over a pile of broken bricks and squeezed under a fallen beam, leaving Lower Quentaris behind. On the other side, rain had claimed the city. It fell in torrents, gushing from overflowing gutters, cascading from roofs, pouring over the cobblestones and turning open drains into major canals. Nisha was drenched in an instant. She slipped and fell into a puddle, sending spray flying. Laughing, she rolled in the water, tilted back her head and let the warm rain fall on her face. 'It's wonderful, Tal!' Water ran into her mouth. She swallowed, choked and laughed. 'The heat has broken, Tal!'

He joined her and together they cheered and stamped in the puddles, kicking up water. The street was full of lunatics doing the same, singing and howling in the downpour. Women, men, boys and girls, staggering around sodden and dripping, but all grinning, laughing and slapping each other on the back.

'Nisha, we're home!'

'Oh yes, Tal!' Nisha shouted. 'What a magical city Quentaris is!'

THE QUENTARIS CHRONICLES

Also by Michael Pryor

Quentaris in Flames

When a fire is deliberately lit in the city of Quentaris, Nisha Fairsight and her minstrel friend Tal investigate and soon uncover a plot threatening its inhabitants. Adding to the city's woes is the threat of invasion from the vicious, insect-like Zolka, who are making it even more dangerous than usual to pass through the rift caves.

Nisha must discover her fire-magic heritage and her place in Quentaris. Will she be able to save the city and her friends?

Michael Pryor is the author of many popular and award-winning novels and short stories, including *Quentaris in Flames*. Michael lives in Melbourne with his wife Wendy and two daughters, Celeste and Ruby.

ISBN 0 7344 0469 7

Swords of Quentaris

Paul Collins

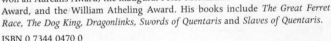

Rad de La'rel is a street urchin who yearns to be a guide to adventurers in the rift caves of Quentaris. But before he can claim his birthright, he must escape the Thieves' Guild and the notorious Vindon Nibhelline with the help of his friend Tulcia. Only then will he be proclaimed the greatest guide since his ancestor, the legendary Nathine de La'rel.

Paul Collins's fiction has been short-listed for many Australian science fiction and fantasy awards. He has won an Aurealis Award, the inaugural Peter McNamara Award, and the William Atheling Award. His books include *The Great Ferret Race*, *The Dog King*, *Dragonlinks*, *Swords of Quentaris* and *Slaves of Quentaris*.

ISBN 0 7344 0470 0

Also by Paul Collins

Slaves of Quentaris

Yukin and his mate, Yulen, flee their campsite when Akcarum slave-traders attack. Unable to escape the Akcarum hunter birds, they are caught and transported to Quentaris. On their journey through the rift caves Yukin discovers a power that taps into the senses of insects and animals. But can it save them in time?

ISBN 0 7344 0557 X

The Perfect Princess

Jenny Pausacker

Tab Vidler is an orphan who works for the Dung Brigade, sweeping the streets of Quentaris. One day she meets a mysterious stranger called Azt Marossa and before long she is helping him escape from the Archon's guards and avoid Duelph and Nibhelline sword fighters. Most importantly of all, she's finding out what really happened to her heroine, the Perfect Princess, who fled Quentaris years ago ...

Jenny Pausacker has written sixty books for young people, from picture books and junior fantasies to science fiction and Young Adult novels, winning several awards. Jenny's titles include *Scam* and *Looking for Blondie* (Crime Waves), and *The Rings* in Lothian's After Dark series.

ISBN 0 7344 0586 3

The Revognase

Lucy Sussex

Life in the city of Quentaris is never dull. The city's two feuding families, the Blues and the Greens, have just held a battle in the market. There has been a duel between wizards and a burglary at the Villains' Guild. And the Chief Soothsayer has just prophesied another disaster: 'I see a disc of changing colours, passing from hand to hand. I see murder, misery and mayhem. I see the disc destroying everyone who touches it!'

Lucy Sussex has been published internationally and in various genres, including children's fiction, literary criticism, horror and crime fiction. She has won the Ditmar and Aurealis Awards, and been short-listed for the Kelly Awards (for crime writing) and the Wilderness Society Environment Award for children's literature.

ISBN 0 7344 0495 6